Déjà Vu Bride

Debra Ullrick

Déjà vu Bride

1st edition published by Spirit Light Publishing 2008
2nd edition
Published by: Sweet Impressions Publishing
Cover by Lynnette Bonner
Image ©BigStock-48847910

Printed in the United States of America

Library of Congress Cataloging-in-Publication Data is available upon request.
ISBN 9780692234358

This book is a work of fiction. Names, characters, places, and incidents are a product of the author's imagination or are used fictitiously. Any resemblance to actual events, locales, or persons, living or dead, is coincidental.

The truth was Erik could get used to having her around. While he wasn't in love with Olivia, he was very attracted to her—and not just physically. There was something about her that drew him. Maybe it was because she seemed lost and alone. Or maybe it was the playful side of her when she knew no one was paying attention. Whatever it was, as he treaded water and watched her swimming, he knew he wanted to pursue it and find out. He also sensed that he needed to go slow and just be her friend first. Plus, he wasn't sure how his being her boss would affect a relationship with her. He needed to be careful to not cross over that line. As she swam froggie-style toward him, one look at her beautiful turquoise eyes and he realized that wasn't going to be easy.

Erik's imagination took over. He pictured Olivia swimming up to him and putting her soft hands on his shoulders. He pulled her into his arms, their eyes locked and held there until his attention drifted to her mouth. Water beads covered her lips. Lips he longed to feel against his own. In slow motion, he leaned his head toward her until their parted mouths met in a warm, wet kiss. Her soft lips played with his, consuming him until...

"What're you doing?" Olivia's unknowing, innocent question yanked Erik back to reality.

Good grief, man. What's wrong with you lately? And what is it about her that has you fantasizing about kissing her? He chanced a quick glance into Olivia's eyes just an arm length away in front of him, wondering how he was going to answer her question.

Sweet Impressions
PUBLISHING

Dedication

This book is dedicated to John Seasock, driver of the Batman monster truck, and two-time Monster Jam World Finals champion in 2007 and 2008. Congratulations, John! Thank you for sharing your expertise with me, for making the monster truck scenes come to life, and for patiently answering my bazillion questions. To learn more about monster trucks visit John's website at www.JohnSeasock.com

Special Thanks To

Staci Stallings. Thank you for believing in me, and for all the boo-coo hours you've spent editing my books, encouraging me, teaching me, and mentoring me. And not just in my writing but in my Christian walk, and life in general. My life is richer and happier because of you. Thanks for constantly directing me to the only One who truly matters. I love you and appreciate you more than words can say.

It is my honor to dedicate the ministry part of this story to you and to Raef. And you know why.

Greg S. Davis, photographer and airbrush painter extraordinaire, thanks for sharing your vast knowledge of airbrush painting with me. To see Greg's beautiful photography and airbrush paintings visit his website at: www.gsdavisphotography.com

Tamarack in Beckley, West Virginia, thank you for the beautiful pictures and valuable information you sent me. I hope I did Tamarack proud. And if I misplaced something, I apologize ahead of time.

Rick Ullrick, thank you, honey, for supporting me and for loving me, even when I was unlovable.

And last, but definitely not least, to my Lord and Savior, Jesus, thank you so much for loving me enough to die for me.

LIFE IS FULL OF CHOICES

When tragedy strikes, we have a choice to turn to God or away from God.

I have set before you life and death, blessing and cursing, therefore choose life.
Deuteronomy 30:19b

Prologue

Olivia Roseman peeled back the curtain and pressed her head against the marred glass of her apartment window. Tears of rain poured down from the dark afternoon sky. She tried to shake the foreboding heaviness that pressed in on her from all sides but it clung to her like a blood-sucking leech. The last time she'd felt like this, something horrible had happened to someone she loved. She could only hope that wasn't the case this time. Too many people she cherished were already dead.

Dead.

That one word sent a tsunami of fresh grief gushing over her, sucking her in to its path of destruction like it had so many times before. She tried hard not to focus on the ominous intruder enshrouding her. But no matter how hard she tried, the bleak cloud of doom lingered like the unwelcome flood waters outside.

Moisture filled her eyes, she blinked it away.

The loud ringing of her telephone jarred her body.

She gawked at the antiquated device as if it were a poisonous snake ready to strike.

Dread, familiar and unwanted, flooded every part of her being.

Four rings later, she knew she couldn't avoid it or the bad news that was certain to come, so she released the tattered gold curtain, letting it fall back into place.

She inched her way toward the phone, gulping in several deep breaths, and forcing as much courage into herself as she could muster.

Receiver in hand, she slowly pressed it against her ear. “Hello.”

“Livvy?”

Olivia’s heart skipped at the familiar breathy voice. “Hammond?” she squealed, pressing the phone tighter to her ear as if that would somehow bring him closer to her.

“No. It’s me. Haskell.” A heavy sigh accompanied his answer.

“Oh.” Disappointment plopped into Olivia’s heart. She braced herself against the dilapidated desk, feeling as if they would both crash to the floor at any moment.

“I’m sorry I haven’t returned any of your calls.” His tone was so soft she barely heard him.

“Why haven’t you?” Olivia knew she sounded perturbed, but the frustration she’d felt every time she called and he “wasn’t available” angered her even through her grief. He was avoiding her, and she wanted to know why.

“I’ll explain it someday, but not right now. Listen, the reason I’m calling is to let you know that I’ve received news about—”

“Hammond,” Olivia blurted, bolting away from the desk. “You have news about Hammond?”

“Yes.”

“What news? What have you heard?”

“I’m afraid it’s not good, Liv. They’ve found Hammond’s plane.”

"Hamm—Hammond's plane?" She put her hand behind her, searching for the wobbly chair, then lowered herself onto its hard surface. The words she never wanted to ask slipped past her tongue in a hoarse whisper. "Is he…?"

"No."

She sat up straight as that one little word sent a spark of hope into her threadbare heart. "He's not dead?"

"I—I don't know. His bod—he wasn't in the plane." The confusion and sadness in Haskell's voice seeped into her, and her heart went out to him.

After all, he and Hammond had been inseparable. When you saw one, the other was likely to be nearby. Born only minutes apart, they shared the same hazel eyes, light brown hair, tiny cleft chin, and low timber voice. This had to be killing him as much as it was her.

Olivia brushed her fingers over her eyes, down her cheeks, and over her chin. While she hated to ask Haskell her next two questions, for her own sanity's sake, she had to know about her missing fiancé. "Then where is he, Haskell, and where did they find his plane?"

"It's lying on the side of Rock Cliff Canyon in Colorado."

Lying on its side? Olivia gulped back the lump forming in her throat. Her soul went numb as she tried to maintain some semblance of sanity long enough to make sense of what he was telling her.

"The officials said the only thing that kept the aircraft from slipping off into the river below were the trees." He sniffed. "They also said…"

The rest of the conversation blurred as Haskell's words sunk in…

…aircraft lying on its side…

…river below…

…body nowhere in sight...

Olivia's stomach heaved.

Her hand flew to her mouth.

She swallowed several times, forcing the burning bile back into her stomach.

This was déjà vu all over again. At ten years old, she'd heard those same words when her parents had flown in their friends' private plane, and it had crashed in the Atlantic Ocean. They'd never found their bodies either.

"No," she whimpered, shaking her head. *Please, not again.* "I'm sorry," she interrupted Haskell. "But I have to go."

"I'm so sorry, Livvy. I know how much you loved him. I did too." Haskell's weepy voice sent Olivia over the edge.

"Good—goodbye." She placed the phone in its cradle, her arms fell limp at her sides.

Crumpling onto the lumpy rollaway bed, she buried her face in her pillow and wept bitter tears.

An eternity later, when there were no more tears left, Olivia rolled over and sat up. Her eyes stung, and her head throbbed. She lifted the picture of Hammond from its home on the rickety nightstand and lovingly ran her fingers over his face. She closed her eyes and clutched the picture to her chest. A lone tear trickled down her cheek.

Oh, Hammond. My precious, Hammond. Why did you

fly when they warned you not to?

She pressed her lips together and shook her head. She knew why.

Hammond loved adventure. At one time, she had too. But her adventurous spirit had disappeared with him. If only he would have listened to her.

If only *God* would have listened to her.

But He hadn't.

The rejection she felt from God not answering her prayer stabbed painful daggers into her soul, slicing it and shredding it until it bled the life out of her. Once again someone she loved had been ripped from her. And once again she was left with the unbearable pain of losing someone she loved.

Her eyes journeyed heavenward. "How could You allow this to happen, God? I trusted You." Olivia didn't even try to keep the anger from her voice. "I did everything right this time. I prayed. I believed. I stood on Your promises. I even called several prayer lines and asked them to agree with me that Hammond would be found safe and sound. And yet You still let him die. Why, Lord? *Why*?"

Just how much more did she have to endure in this lifetime? Or more to the point, how much more *could* she endure without completely falling apart?

Olivia jerked the picture away from her chest and slammed it face down on the nightstand. The piercing crack echoed in the room. Pain sliced through her already throbbing head. She raised the picture and turned it over, marveling at how her life resembled the mess staring back at her, broken, shattered, and beyond repair.

Her eyes stung as if someone had scraped sandpaper across them. On weak legs, she wobbled the few steps to her bathroom and opened the rinky-dink linen cabinet. The only hinge holding it together broke loose, and it flew from her hand and landed in the turquoise bathtub. The reverberating bang caused her head to throb even worse. Olivia closed her eyes. What else could possibly go wrong?

She grabbed a washcloth, turned the spigot, and placed the shabby cloth under the running water. Her gaze snagged on her reflection in the mirror. Red blotches dotted her face and puffy bloodshot eyes stared back at her.

Several wobbly turns of the sprocket-like sink handle and the water stopped running, except for the perpetual, irritating drip. Olivia squeezed the excess water from the washcloth, pressed it against her eyes, and allowed the coolness to seep into them.

Minutes later when warmth replaced the coolness in the washrag, she folded it and laid it in on the rim of her sink. She reached for the Tylenol bottle, dumped three pills in her hand, and set it back on her makeshift shelf above the washbasin. A cockroach scurried by her hand, and she jerked back. “Ewww. Gross.” Olivia cringed as she watched the disgusting invader fall over the edge and into the rust-stained sink. No matter how long she lived in this dive, she never got used to the bugs or the gross, irremovable lime deposits from previous tenants, the peeled wallpaper, cracked linoleum, brown stained 70’s orange and gold carpet or the musty smell.

This repulsive place was just another reminder of her unanswered prayers—of God’s abandonment of her. Right then and there, Olivia determined to live her life without God's aid; and she'd start right now by making some drastic changes. "Goodbye, Wheeling. Hello, Charity, West Virginia."

Chapter One

Erik Cole stepped around the corner at Cole Chevrolet and sucked in a sharp breath. He stopped so abruptly that he almost bumped into himself. *Woo wee. Surely she isn't my next appointment.* He should have paid closer attention when his secretary had told him about his two o'clock. But no-o, his mind had been on the next monster truck race down in Shreveport, Louisiana. As far as he knew his interview was with some guy named Ollie. This gal was definitely no Ollie. His heart shifted into high gear.

Glancing around to make sure no one else was watching him, he peeked through the glass door and took in the sight of her. With her back ramrod straight and her arms crossed, she stared at the wall. Her light caramel colored hair ran past her shoulders, over her elbows, and down to her waist, reminding him of a waterfall. Unlike some of the sickeningly skinny models on the cover of Monster Truck Magazine, this gal was round and shapely and had curves in all the right places.

"Why don't you go in and introduce yourself?"

Erik jumped. Heat rose from his neck all the way to his scalp. He turned and faced his mom's sister. "Hi, Aunt Adell. To what do I owe the pleasure of this visit?" He smiled tenderly at his favorite aunt, who resembled his mother with her long bangs blending into a shoulder length, flip style hair-do and her smiling brown eyes. Eyes so like his mother's and his other three siblings. How he missed his family. Times like this, he questioned the sanity of moving from Alabama to West Virginia. But he had grown so tired of the everyday ho-hum of his job and had craved some challenge in his life. West Virginia had definitely proven to be a challenge—in more ways than one.

But it wasn't just boredom and the need for a challenge that had caused him to make the drastic move. Shortly after his sister Camara's wedding, a restlessness had developed in his spirit and he knew God was about to ask Him to do something big. When he attended the monster truck rally at the Charleston Civic Center, the friendly people and the rugged beauty of his mother's birth state had reeled him in. That, and a "knowing" in his spirit that a move to West Virginia was the answer to his restlessness. So, before he knew it, he'd said goodbye to his precious family and Swamper City, Alabama, and moved to Charity, West Virginia, where he joined the wonderful, proud family of mountaineers.

Inwardly he chuckled. One of the first things his aunt had warned him about was to never call West Virginians hillbillies, but mountaineers. The second thing she'd told him was, contrary to popular belief, most West Virginians were not a bunch of backward uneducated hillbillies. That most were indeed well-educated and very Godly. Although he had only lived here for a brief while, he had to agree with his aunt. The people here did their best to make Erik feel welcome and a part of their family. As hard as they tried though, it still wasn't the same as having his own family around. He especially missed his little sister

Camara. His chest heaved with loneliness for her.

His aunt must have sensed his homesickness because she set the tin box on his outer office window ledge and wrapped her arms around him in a motherly hug. Cinnamon and spice filled his nostrils.

"You miss your family, don't you?"

Erik smiled and slowly nodded. "I do. But having you around makes me less homesick."

"Oh tootles." She waved his comment away, blushing.

Erik nervously glanced over his shoulder.

Her attention followed his. "Who's that little beauty?"

"She's my next appointment."

"Well, then. I'd better not keep you." The tinkling lilt in his aunt's voice and the twinkle in her eye gave evidence to the fact that somehow she knew he was attracted to the long-haired beauty sitting in his outer office. Was he that transparent? Or was it something about older women that they could read minds? Whatever it was, it made him nervous. He didn't want people knowing his private thoughts.

She reached for the tin and handed it to him. "I just stopped by to give you these. I thought you might enjoy some pumpkin-apple cookies. They were your mother's favorite." She patted his cheek and brushed the one rebellious strand of his hair that constantly fell across his forehead back into place just like his mother used to. "You know every time I see you, your hair gets a little bit darker. The same thing happened to your uncle. My brother's hair was buttercup yellow when he was young, and now it's dark brown like yours. Must come with age." She winked and smiled. "Well, I'd better go." She peered over his shoulder. "Whatever you do, don't let that one get away." With that, his aunt spun around and skittered down the corridor.

Erik raked his fingers through his hair and rubbed the back of his neck. In the short time he'd lived here, he'd learned two things about Aunt Adell. One—she was a great judge of character. Two—her female intuition was impeccable.

Well then, he glanced down at his burgundy shirt, balanced the cookie tin in one hand, and quickly tucked his shirttail in. He'd better get to it. After wiping the dust off of his pressed blue jeans, he laid a spearmint breath strip on his tongue and opened the door.

Terri rose from her chair behind her wooden desk. "It's about time you got here," his matronly secretary whispered.

"Sorry, I'm late. I got delayed," he spoke loud enough so that the woman waiting for him could hear him too.

At the sound of his voice, the lady turned.

Erik's lungs ceased to work.

One word came to mind. Stunning.

"Mr. Cole, this is Miss Roseman."

The word "Miss" snagged his attention. He kept his smile from showing even though his stomach was doing a ten point, monster truck cyclone. He took three long strides toward her, shifted the cookie tin to his left hand, and extended his right hand. "Nice to meet you, Miss Roseman."

When her soft hand touched his, sparks flew up his

arm. Thunderstruck, he cleared his throat and released her hand.

"Please, call me Olivia." Her raspy voice punctured his inner core. He'd always been a sucker for a woman with a broken husky voice.

Their eyes connected.

Turquoise eyes, unlike anything he'd ever seen before, threatened to draw him into their depths.

C'mon Erik. Pull yourself together man. This is an interview for a job, not a date.

Erik strong-armed himself to look away and turned toward Terri. "Hold all my calls, okay?"

"I sure will." Her brown eyes sparkled behind her oval glasses.

He wanted to warn his secretary to behave, but not in front of Miss Roseman. This time he'd let her not-so-subtle matchmaking notion go.

"Miss Rose—, Olivia. Shall we go into my office?" He motioned toward the door.

She picked up her portfolio, gave him a small smile, and nodded.

As she walked past him, the scent of roses floated up his nostrils. *Man she smells nice*. He glanced at the ripples of gold threading their way down her waist length tresses. His fingers itched to touch one of the curls to see if they were as soft as they looked. *Oh man,* Erik groaned inwardly, then gave himself another good talking to. *Stop it! This is ridiculous. You're a grown man, not some love struck high school boy. So stop acting like one.*

Lord, help me to get through this interview. And if

she's the one You want me to hire, please show me. I want Your will, not mine.

♥♥♥

If Olivia were still a praying woman, she'd pray her heart out for the strength to make it through this interview. But she wasn't. Unfortunately, she knew she was on her own with this one. The second she laid eyes on the handsome man, she battled the urge to stare at him. She hadn't expected the employer to be quite so good-looking. Nor had she expected her pulse to increase.

A good seven inches taller than her, he sported her favorite combination—dark brown hair and brown eyes. Large chocolate disks came to mind. And the miniscule cleft in his chin gave his face a strong masculine appeal.

Olivia stepped inside his office. Her eyes locked onto several pictures of people and trucks hanging on the pale blue wall.

"Have a seat." Mr. Cole motioned toward a cornflower blue chair.

Olivia willed her insides to stop shaking, but they weren't cooperating. "Thank you." When she sat down, the leather chair squeaked, filling the silence. She crossed her legs and watched him lower his tall, broad shouldered frame onto a navy chair on the opposite side of the expansive desk.

He set a tin canister off to the side, leaned forward, placed his arms on the desk, and folded his large hands together. Hands so like Hammond's. *Not now, Olivia! This is* not *the time or the place to think about Hammond.* Olivia forced all thoughts of Hammond from her mind and concentrated on the man who was about to interview her.

"So, you're interested in painting my monster truck?"

"Yes." Olivia hated that her voice shook. Too bad it was unprofessional to chew gum during an interview because right now she longed to pop a whole pack in her mouth. Gum chewing had a way of calming her nerves.

"Do you have any experience?"

"Yes." She glanced down at her portfolio, unzipped it, and then looked up at him. "I've airbrush painted a few trucks and hundreds of motorbikes and snowmobiles before."

That is before Hammond disappeared, and before her ex-boss, Markus, decided to try and force himself on her. Thankfully, Rob, one of her coworkers had come back to the shop to get something he'd forgotten or otherwise… Olivia contained the shudder that rippled through her.

Since that dreadful day, her ex-boss had sabotaged every chance she had of gaining employment in Wheeling. He said he would get even with her, and he had. Humph. Like it was *her* fault that Markus had been arrested for attacking her. To this day, she still couldn't believe that her ex-boss had actually accused her of leading him on. Of flirting with him and teasing him. But Olivia knew that wasn't true because she only had eyes for Hammond. Even after Hammond's disappearance.

Besides, something about the way Markus had always looked at her made her skin crawl. Olivia had gone out of her way to avoid him, and only talked to him when she absolutely had to. And each time she spoke with him, she'd kept it strictly business. So his accusations about it being her fault were definitely false. Markus just wanted someone to blame for his repulsive action.

Too bad she had to put her ex-boss down for a reference.

Overwhelmed with the prospect that Markus could somehow jeopardize her chances of landing employment here as well, Olivia thought about asking God to help her get this job, and to not have Mr. Cole call Markus for a reference, but she knew He wasn't listening to her. So why bother? Instead, she crossed her fingers, hoping Mr. Cole wouldn't ask for any references.

As she shifted her portfolio on her lap, to her horror the laminated pictures slipped from her grasp and cascaded to the floor. "Oh no." She tossed her leather case on his desk and scooted off the chair. Squatting, she grabbed four pictures and shuffled them in an even stack. When she reached for her eagle drawing, her hand landed on top of Mr. Cole's. Her gaze flew upward and snagged onto his. Olivia found herself helpless to break contact. His rain-fresh aftershave drifted up her nose.

"I've got it." His deep voice mingled with spearmint snapped her out of her trance. Not one to blush, Olivia felt her cheeks flame. She jerked her hand away and dropped her head. Grateful her long hair curtained her face, she forced herself to not look at him but instead focused her attention on the other drawings still sprawled across the floor.

While she gathered the three closest to her, Mr. Cole

scooped up the remaining ones about three feet away from her and stood. With his free hand, he gently clutched her elbow and helped her up.

"I'm so sorry." She took the pictures from him and turned to gather her case from off his desk. "I should have—." Her mouth dropped open in horror. "Oh no," she groaned. How could she have been so stupid? Why didn't she look before tossing her case? She scrambled to find something to wipe up the dark liquid sprawling across the end of his desk. She spotted a box of tissues, jerked several out and started blotting the spill. The tissues shredded the instant they touched the liquid, leaving oodles of tiny particles and making an even bigger mess.

He laid his hand on her arm.

Olivia refused to look at him. She'd never been so mortified in her life.

"Please, don't worry about it."

Tears stung the backs of her eyes at the kindness in his voice, but she refused to cry. She gathered what she could of the muddle she had made and tossed it into a nearby trashcan.

He pushed the intercom button. "Terri, would you bring some paper towels in here, please?"

Within seconds, the door opened and in bustled the tiny middle-aged woman. Olivia extended her hand toward her so she could take the roll and clean up her monstrous mess.

Terri waved her away. "I'll get it." She unrolled several of the towels. "This happens all the time." His secretary darted a glance at Erik and then back at her.

Olivia forced her mouth shut and stared at the woman whose smile reminded her of her mother's. Loneliness threatened to overshadow her as it so often did when she thought about her mother. Would the pain of missing her mom ever go away? Not a day went by that Olivia wished she would have treated her mother and father better. But she hadn't. If only… *No! I won't think about that now. I won't.*

Within seconds Terri had the disaster wiped clean. She tossed the paper towels in a trashcan and looked at Olivia. "I keep telling him he needs one of them spill-proof cups." His secretary wrinkled her button nose at Mr. Cole. "I guess I'll have to take money out of petty cash and go get you one." She looked at Olivia and winked.

Then, as fast as she'd breezed in, she breezed out. And Olivia was left alone to face her humiliation. She sucked in her lower lip and drew in a long breath as she gathered enough courage to face him.

Light pressure on her shoulder caused her to look sideways and up into his face. The compassion and understanding she saw in his eyes touched a chord somewhere deep in her soul. A place she wasn't willing to explore.

"It's okay." He smiled, showing a row of white even teeth with the exception of one slightly crooked one on the upper left side. "Please," he motioned toward the chair she'd occupied just minutes before. "Have a seat while I take a look at your drawings."

"Thank you." She dipped her head. Seeing the coffee-stained papers and desk calendar, she again apologized. "I really am sorry."

"Forget it. No harm done." He grabbed some papers and a calendar with monster truck photos and then sat back down in his office chair. He picked up her drawings and started looking through them.

While he studied the pictures, Olivia scarcely breathed. After the mess she'd made, she wondered if she had completely blown any chance she might have had of getting hired. If only she believed in prayer, this would be a good time for it. But she didn't. In fact, she wasn't even sure she believed in God anymore.

♥♥♥

"These are really good." Erik laid the picture of a bald eagle with its wings spread on top of the rest of her drawings and looked at her.

The uncertainty in her eyes crushed him. Maybe that look stemmed from the spilled coffee incident. If she only knew the number of times he himself had done stuff like that. Without knowing for sure why she looked that way, he opted to ignore it rather than risk embarrassing her by asking. "Would you like something to drink?"

Her eyes widened, and she gave him a, you're-kidding look. "No thank you, Mr. Cole."

"Mr. Cole?" Erik smiled and chuckled. "Please, call me Erik. Mr. Cole makes me feel old."

"Okay." She hesitated. "Erik."

He liked the way his name sounded through her broken voice.

"Are these original creations? I mean did you design these yourself?" *Please say yes.* He wanted to keep her around.

"Yes, sir. I did."

His insides relaxed. "Nix the 'sir'. Just Erik, okay?"

She nodded and sucked in her lower lip.

"Listen." He leaned forward and clasped his hands in front of him. "I know most monster truck drivers have gone to shrink wrap for their fiberglass bodies, but that's not for me. What I'm looking for is someone to not only paint the numerous monster truck bodies I'll wreck, but to also redesign the one I already have. I have three trucks, but I only need one design for all of them."

Her eyes brightened. "I can do that." The confidence in her tone did funny things to his insides.

He admired confident women. Especially this one.

"Do you have a name already picked out for your truck?" She uncrossed her legs and leaned forward.

"Yes. The Mad Masher."

"I see."

Erik saw the wheels in her head turning.

"What style of body?"

"A '71 Chevy pickup."

She nodded. "How much detail are you wanting? I mean, do you want a flashy picture, a simple one, or what did you have in mind?"

"Well." He leaned back in his chair and clasped his hands behind his head. "I love blue. So I want the truck to be mostly in blues except of course for the name and whatever design it has."

"Okay." Her gaze went to his office wall. She tapped her finger against her lips and scrunched her face as she studied the pictures of his monster truck leaping over smashed cars, buses, and motor homes. "I know." Her eyes widened. "How about putting a replica of your truck, leaping in the air over crushed cars on each door? I can make the bottom of the tires look as if they're alive and devouring the obstacles they're leaping over. You know, kind of like the curl of an ocean wave." She squinted and pursed her lips. "The grill of the truck could have a wicked grin and sinister eyes. The body could be in a medium shade of blue with navy tire tread stripes down the sides and the drawing of the truck could be white. Your name and the name of the truck could be in dark blue outlined with white."

The way she described it, Erik could visualize it in his mind. And he liked what he saw. She made it come to life, unlike the others he had interviewed before her. He'd like nothing more than to hire her on the spot, but he wouldn't do it without consulting God first. The Lord's will meant more to him than his own. Erik sent up a silent request asking God to make it clear if he was to hire her. He no sooner asked the Lord than a resounding yes dropped into his spirit.

"Olivia. You've got yourself a job. When can you start?"

Her mouth formed an O. "I, um..."

"I'm sorry. How foolish of me. We haven't even discussed wages, hours, or what all you'd be doing." After talking over the preliminaries with her, Erik couldn't keep the hope-filled look from his face as he stared at her, waiting for her answer. Not only did he find her extremely attractive, she was talented too. Of all the people he'd interviewed, her work was the most impressive.

After several long moments of silence, he had to say something. "If that doesn't work for you, I'm sure we can come up with some sort of an agreement that will."

She waved her hand. "No, no that's fine."

"When can you start?"

The color siphoned from her face. She squirmed in her seat. "Um, I'm not sure. I'd have to find a place to live first."

"Right now it's virtually impossible to find a place around here. But I have a solution if you're interested." The skeptical look in her turquoise eyes made him hasten forward. "I have an empty guest house at my place."

Her brows rose, and she shook her head. "Oh, no. I couldn't do that. I'm sure I can find something." The look of uncertainty touched a chord deep within him.

He leaned back in his chair. "Listen. You'd be doing me a favor. My housekeeper is tired of airing out the place. The way I see it, the house would be better off with someone living in it, and you need a place to live. It's a perfect solution for both of us. Plus, the shop you'll be working in is close to the cottage. Why drive fifteen miles when you can live right there? I know this sounds selfish, but it really would help my housekeeper and me out. What d' ya say?"

♥♥♥

Olivia pulled in her lower lip. She stared into the air, contemplating what to do. While she had planned on living in her car, she now realized the futility of that because she'd have to eat out and pay for a shower somewhere until she got paid.

Mentally she ticked off her options, or lack thereof.

First off, her biggest road block was her financial situation. Her measly few dollars wouldn't go very far.

Secondly, most people required the first and last month's rent.

Thirdly, if she got a motel, it would cost at least forty dollars a day. And usually hotels that cheap were in the sleaziest, most dangerous neighborhoods. She'd had enough of that.

Plus, she'd need fuel to drive back and forth to work every day. Again, money she didn't have.

Mr. Cole said there wasn't anything available. She knew that to be true because she'd checked on the Internet at the library before she came here. The few places she'd seen available were for sale only. That definitely left her out.

A piece of gum sounded great about now.

She continued to weigh her options.

If she stayed at his guesthouse, he insisted she'd be helping him and his housekeeper out. And if she did, she wouldn't have to leave her beloved cat Samson behind.

She looked up at Erik and studied his face. There was nothing in his eyes that creeped her out or frightened her like Markus' had.

What choice did she have really? Her only logical option was to take Mr. Cole up on his offer. At least until she got her first paycheck anyway. Then she would reassess her situation and maybe do something else. *Well*, she sighed, *here goes nothing*. Pulling in a breath of courage, she stood.

Erik followed suit.

Finally, she looked at him, extended her hand, and smiled. “You’ve got yourself a deal.”

“Great.” The stiffness in his stance, relaxed. He glanced at his watch. “Listen, I’m pretty much done for the day, so why don’t I take you out there now to show you my truck? The shop you’ll be working in and the cottage are within walking distance of each other. Will that work for you?”

Knowing that any other choices were non-existent at this point, she swallowed the small lump of fear caught in her throat. “Yes, that’ll be fine. I just need to gather the rest of my drawings.” Along with a mega dose of courage. She was definitely going to need it.

Chapter Two

Olivia walked alongside Erik. Outside, beads of moisture that had nothing to do with June's warm weather pooled across her nose. She removed the threadbare hanky her grandmother had made, dabbed her nose and forehead, then slipped the embroidered cloth back into place.

Everything was happening so fast, her mind whirled. Not only had she just acquired a job doing what she loved most, she would also have a new place to live. A cottage. Olivia wondered what it looked like and if it was furnished. Any place had to be better than her current residence. In spite of her trepidation of having to live near her new boss, thoughts of seeing her new home—even if it was temporary—sent excitement dancing through her veins.

"Where are you parked?" Even his voice was nice.

Olivia squinted against the brightness and looked up at him. Erik stepped in front of her, blocking the sun. Nice, good looking, thoughtful, and a gentleman too. All the things she had loved in Hammond. She hated how thoughts of Hammond would ambush her at the worst possible times. *Stop thinking about him. It's been over a year since he disappeared. You're here to make a fresh, clean break, remember?* She drew up her shoulders. "Over there." Olivia pointed toward her vehicle. "The '68 Nova."

Erik's gaze followed to where she pointed. "Nice."

She stared at her purple metal-flecked car. With its Keystone wheels and spinners, wide white raised lettered tires, Gabriel High Jacker raised rear-end, and spacers on the front, she wondered if the man standing next to her, who owned a Chevrolet dealership and could buy whatever car he wanted saw a classic car or a piece of junk.

"My sister, Camara, loves classic cars. Especially Chevys. So whatever you do, don't let her see that little beauty. She'll try to talk you into selling it to her."

Hearing what he thought of her pride and joy, Olivia's heart smiled. Even though she had a hard time getting the car started sometimes, she still loved it.

"Well, I'll go get my truck and meet you here. Then you can follow me out of town, okay?"

Follow him? Olivia's heart gained momentum. Being directionally challenged had often placed her in precarious situations. She started to panic at the idea of getting lost. But then she reminded herself that she had found her way to Charity without any problems. Thanks to her best friend Audra, who had printed a map from the Internet that gave her step-by-step directions that even a child could follow. Olivia hated to admit it, but without the detailed map she would have definitely gotten lost.

As he walked away, Olivia studied the tall, handsome man, with the broad shoulders and lean waist. She admired the way he carried himself; it oozed confidence. With a sigh, she headed toward her car.

Thank goodness Mr. Cole didn't ask her to ride to his place with him. The very idea made her uncomfortable. She wasn't sure if it was because in some small way he reminded her of Hammond, or if it was the idea of being stuck in such close proximity with the handsome stranger, who was now her boss.

Memories of her ex-boss, Markus and his lust-filled eyes when he forced her down onto the couch and tore at her shirt flashed through her mind. Olivia pinched her eyes shut and quivered. As hard as she tried, she couldn't shake the fear that came every time the memory resurfaced. If only Hammond would have been there, he would have beaten that man within one inch of his life. But he wasn't—then—or now. And because of that, things would never be the same again.

Her chest rose and fell. What she'd give to feel safe and secure and well provided for again. Like when her parents were alive. Or when Hammond was aliv—

Enough, Olivia! Stop it, already. Let the past go. Hammond's never coming back, and Markus can't ever hurt you again. You finally got a great paying job with a really nice boss. At least she thought he was nice. He didn't appear to be anything like Markus. Markus had an aura of evil, and his eyes used to glaze over her body, undressing her. Whereas Erik's eyes didn't touch her body, and the man radiated peace, kindness, and gentleness.

Once she reached her car, she put the key in the door and jiggled it until it unlocked. She slid behind the wheel, put the clutch in, and turned the key. The Nova's glass pac mufflers rumbled from the engine's power. A sound she loved and never tired of. Smiling, Olivia pulled the seat belt over her lap and clicked it shut. One glance at her near-empty gas gauge, and her smile evaporated. *Oh no.* She closed her eyes and blew out a short breath.

Mentally she calculated how much money she had left. The weight of her dire situation pressed in on her, but she slapped it aside.

Sleeping in her car wouldn't be so bad. After all, she'd done it before.

She rolled down her window to let in fresh air. Times like this, she wished she could afford air conditioning. Hopefully this evening it would be cool and her car wouldn't be so hot and stuffy. But even if it was, too bad, so sad. If she had to sleep in her car, then so be it. She'd just deal with it.

She looked in her rearview mirror, then backed out and waited for Erik. A dark blue Chevy extended cab pickup with a lift kit and big tires pulled along side her.

Erik hopped out and came around to her door. "I didn't think to ask you before. Are you okay with following me, or would you like to ride with me and pick up your car later?"

"No!" she blurted, then quickly struggled to gather her scattering nerves. "I mean, no, I'd much rather drive." She forced a smile onto her face. "How far is your place?"

"A little over fifteen miles."

Olivia squirmed. "Um, I need to get fuel first."

"No problem." He smiled, melting away her discomfort. He sprinted over to his truck and hopped in. Leaning his head out the window, he hollered, "Follow me."

Again with the follow me thing. Olivia swallowed a gulp of fear. "I can do this," she whispered with more confidence than she felt.

When he pulled onto the road, Olivia rammed the gas pedal and stayed close behind him. Glued to his every move, she followed him to a nearby station. Not an economy one either. Yikes!

He pulled ahead of the gas pump and stopped. Olivia drove her car as close to the pump as she could without hitting it. She glanced at the high fuel price, and her spirits fell. Ten cents more a gallon than what she'd paid in Wheeling.

Too embarrassed to let on about her miserable financial situation, Olivia shut off her car and dug around in her large tote bag in search of her billfold. Her hair fell in the way of her search. She gathered her tresses, twisted them, and tossed the mass over her shoulder. Wallet in hand, she pulled out a small bill. She opened her door and stepped out only to find Erik already pumping fuel.

Oh no. Her heart sank lower than the fuel in her tank. How could she tell him to only put in ten dollars worth without completely humiliating herself?

She cleared her throat. "Um, thank you. I'll take over now." Olivia sent what she hoped was a confident smile and reached for the nozzle.

"No, ma'am. I've got it." He flashed her a bright smile.

Dread and humiliation bombarded her. She watched the numbers on the gas pump roll upward. When it reached $14.62 she decided she could forgo dinner.

The numbers kept rolling.

When it finally stopped, Olivia swallowed hard,

walked back to her car, and grabbed her purse. The two apples she'd purchased from a road side stand would have to tide her over until she got back to Wheeling tomorrow. Then she could cook up a batch of Ramen noodles until her last unemployment check arrived. What timing. Her last check would arrive in three days, and now she had a job. Audra would call that a God-thing. But Olivia no longer believed in God. Well, not the loving, caring God Audra spoke of anyway. The God Olivia once loved wasn't loving, caring, or giving. Quite the contrary. At least in her life. Fed up with dwelling in the frustratingly familiar pit of despair and self-pity, Olivia drew in a long breath. She was going to win at the game of life. Without love. And without God's help.

A warm hand touched her shoulder. With a jerk of her head, she gazed up her new boss.

"Your money's no good here." He smiled.

Olivia straightened and looked him in the face. "Excuse me?"

"It's an old saying." His smile widened. "Your money is no good here because your fuel's already been paid for."

"What?" Olivia gasped. "I can't let you do that!" She quickly read the amount again, snatched up her purse, and dug around the bottom, hoping to find more change.

But he just laughed and headed for his truck. "If you're going to follow me, you'd better come on."

Olivia followed his voice and did a double take. Erik was already inside his pickup and had the engine running. Lightning fast, she shoved everything back into her purse and tossed it on the passenger floorboard. She slid behind the wheel and started her car. She'd worry about paying him later. Right now, she wanted to make sure she wasn't left behind.

In between keeping her eye on Erik's truck and the road, her gaze snagged on the beautiful mountain laurel blooms and redbud trees that dotted several people's yards.

After driving several miles, Erik slowed down and turned. Beautiful maple trees lined both sides of the long lane. They rounded a corner where a large white house with dark blue trim stood, looking out of place amidst West Virginia's rugged landscape. The whole place looked like something one would find along the ocean coastlines. Not here in Charity, West Virginia.

One of the first things she noticed was there weren't any flowers other than the two Rhododendron bushes on either side of his porch. Either her new boss was a bachelor, or his wife didn't care for flowers.

Keeping Erik's truck in view, she continued to take in the sights. Off to the side of the main entrance, the building protruded like a bullet with a skylight on top. Next to it stood a large sculptured bush that instantly reminded Olivia of the ceremonial guards in front of Buckingham Palace in England—stock still and unmovable.

On the left, several feet from the sidewalk stood a lone white birch tree. Red rocks surrounded the base of the tree in the shape of a—Olivia did a double take. A monster truck! She laughed. The bright green of the well-manicured lawn really showed off the shape of the monster truck.

Erik followed the driveway around back. On her right was a closed-in swimming pool. Through the large glass windows, Olivia noticed the tile around the pool was light blue and the deck chairs were dark blue. Her boss wasn't kidding when he said he liked blue. That was an understatement.

Olivia continued to follow him around the driveway. Several yards down, on her left, she noticed a gorgeous white house with dark blue trim. She darted her gaze back and forth between the house and following Erik, wondering if that was where she would be living. Surely that wasn't the place he'd mentioned. That huge house was no cottage. On the right, and up about a hundred yards stood a large white metal shop with blue trim. "More blue," she whispered through a chuckle.

Erik stopped in front of the smaller of two large metal buildings hundreds of yards apart. Olivia pulled her car behind his truck and shut the motor off. His long legs preceded him as he hopped out of his pickup. A few steps and he was at her car, opening her door, and extending his hand to her. Hesitant, but not wanting to appear rude, she laid her hand in his. Upon contact, her heart ricocheted against her ribs. She quickly removed her hand from his and stepped out.

"This is where you'll be working." He smiled. "C'mon. I'll show you around."

Falling in step beside him as he headed toward the smallest of the three doors, Olivia's eyes quickly took in the other two doors. They were certainly wide and tall.

Erik unlocked the door, slipped his hand in, and clicked the light on. He moved aside and motioned for her to precede him.

Olivia stepped inside the shop and stopped. Her breath vanished, her eyes darted open, and her mouth formed a wide O. Mere yards in front of her was the most amazing monstrous truck she'd ever seen. Because it was the only one inside the building, she knew it had to be Erik's 1971 Chevrolet monster truck. The one he said she'd be working on. The very idea that she would have the privilege of working on the massive beast sent shivers of delight racing throughout her whole body.

She felt a tap on her shoulder and spun toward it.

"Are you okay?" he asked, his eyes wide but smiling.

She tore her gaze away from the heart-thumping vision in front of her. "Yes, I'm fine. Why?"

"Well, I asked if you wanted to see the shop."

Heat rushed into her cheeks. "Sorry, I didn't hear you. I was too busy admiring your truck. I can't believe I get to paint it." Her inside child rose to the surface, and she smiled up at him.

He returned her smile with a pleased one of his own. "You can get closer. It might be big, but I promise it won't bite."

"I wouldn't care if it did. It's amazing." Without waiting for him, she closed the distance between her and the truck, eyeing it up and down. She guessed it to be about ten feet tall. Her gaze fell to the wheels. "Look at the size of these tires. How big are they anyway?" she asked, placing her hands in the grooves, which made her hands look small in comparison.

"They're sixty-six by forty-three by twenty-five."

Erik stepped between the front and rear tires.

Olivia followed him, and they both looked up through the webbing of the frame at the massive engine. "What size engine does this thing have?"

"It's a Chevy 540 cubic inch, about fifteen hundred horsepower, with an 8-71 blower, spinning ten percent overdriven." He glanced down at Olivia. Her confused look must have shown because his next words were, "Sorry, I get carried away. Monster trucks have a way of doing that to me."

"I can see why." Olivia couldn't keep the awe from her voice. She glanced around the large building. "Where are the other two trucks?"

"In the mechanic shop with my pit crew. They're wrenching them."

Olivia tilted her head sideways. "Wrenching them?"

"Yeah, working on them."

Confused, she scanned the large building that could house ten monster trucks easily.

"I didn't want the guys smelling paint fumes and getting sick," he answered as if he'd read her mind. "Somehow I don't see the men wearing paint masks to work on the trucks."

"Somehow I think you're right." She chuckled.

"I'll introduce them to you later."

Nerves at the prospect of meeting strangers… all men… made her stomach twist into knots.

"Don't worry. They're a bunch of good ol' boys. Some are a little rough around the edges, but a guy couldn't ask for harder or better workers. Too bad you won't see them much. I keep them pretty busy, either out here or in the shop at Cole Chevrolet."

The knots loosened. "Oh. I see." She smiled. Eager to see the rest of the truck, she worked her way toward the back of it, asking Erik questions about the undercarriage and what everything was. With each answer, her enthusiasm grew. Excitement was something she hadn't felt in more days than she could remember.

Olivia's gaze snagged on the airbrush tools. Her eyes widened. Erik had all of the latest equipment. She walked over to the bench and started looking through the stuff. She ran her fingers over the brand new compressor and smiled. What a welcome change it would be. Newer compressors were much quieter than the old ones.

Rows and rows of paints, clear coat, turpentine, paint thinners, and other solvents used to clean the nozzles, the needles; airbrush heads, and other things lined the shelves. Plus all the other stuff she needed to work through the different design layers. Various sized rolls of masking tape, a huge roll of clear Frisk masking film, jars to hold the paint, paint guns, you name it, Erik had it.

She picked up a spray regulator, and to her horror, her stomach growled so loud she thought the whole neighborhood heard it. Her ears and face matched the cherry-red lettering on the side of a paint can. She shot her boss an embarrassed look and smiled sheepishly. "Sorry. It's been a long time since breakfast."

Erik chuckled. "I'm hungry too. Let's go get something to eat. And after that I can show you the cottage."

Her happy moment splintered. Panic snaked through

her mind. There was no way she could afford supper. Olivia held up her hand and shook her head. "No, no, that's okay. I can wait."

"Well, I can't. C'mon." Erik put out his hand to lead her outside where he opened the passenger side door on his pickup.

Now what? What could she say? Before she had a chance to come up with a good excuse, Erik lifted her up and seated her inside. She turned her legs in, and Erik shut the door. No turning back now. Her only option was to eat the cheapest thing on the menu.

But what if he took her to one of those expensive restaurants? Her panic escalated and breathing became difficult. She struggled with what to do. While she still had the gas money Erik had refused, she didn't know how much a meal would cost. How embarrassing it would be to have him wait while she washed dishes to pay for her meal. Did that stuff really happen in real life, or was that only in the movies? Olivia didn't really want to find out, but that didn't stop the thoughts from racing through her brain like an out-of-control racecar as he climbed into the other side.

"A penny for your thoughts?" he asked as he started his truck.

Make that enough pennies to pay for a meal and you've got yourself a deal. At this point she'd even settle for the penny. "I'll take it." She forced her lips to curl upward.

Erik stretched his left leg out and dug into his pant's pocket.

Her brows slipped under her bangs. "I was just

kidding."

"Nope. A deal's a deal." He pulled out several coins. "Here." Erik reached for her hand and turned her palm upward, then dumped the change there. "Surely there's a penny in there somewhere. On second thought whatever's there, it's yours. Now spill."

Olivia moved to hand it back to him, but he tucked his free hand away from her.

"Oh, no. A deal's a deal, remember?"

What was it about this man that put her so at ease?

Not able to help herself, Olivia shook her head and chuckled. "Well, if you're going to be technical about it." She dug through the change, retrieved a penny. "There. I took a penny. Here's your change." When he didn't take it, Olivia laid it on the seat next to him.

Erik shook his head. "Keep it. A thought is worth more than a penny anyway." He put his truck in gear.

The smile vanished from her face. All joking aside, what was she going to tell him? *Oh yeah, by the way, I'm so poor that even a ninety-nine cent hot dog would be stretching my budget.* A light bulb moment flashed through her brain. "I was thinking." She sat up straight in the cab, and Erik cast a glance her way. "I have two apples in my car. Why don't I get them, and we can share them? Then I can grab a bite to eat on my way out of town."

He jerked his head toward her and gave her a you've-got-to-be-kidding-me look. "Thanks for the offer, but Mickie would kill me if I did that. Listen, you've got to help me out here." Erik backed the truck up, turned it around, and followed the driveway the way they'd come. "I know I should've asked you first, but when you agreed to come out here, I called Mickie and asked her to make us something because I didn't know how long it would take to show you around. And if it doesn't get eaten, she'll be a grump for the rest of the evening." He glanced at her. His eyes and smile hinted of his teasing. "Besides, you wouldn't want all that food to go to waste now, would ya?"

In spite of her pathetically humiliating circumstances, how could she resist that hopeful, sheepish look? Besides, once again, he'd come to her rescue. She inhaled a sigh of relief and exhaled the pent-up anxiety. "No. I guess not." She smiled as her growling stomach thanked her.

"Thanks. You're a lifesaver."

No, you are.

"So, you're planning on going back to Wheeling tonight?"

"Yes." Her original plan had been to sleep in a motel. Then she decided to sleep in her car and save her meager funds. But the more she'd thought about sleeping in her car in a strange town, the more she decided it would be best if she made the trip back to Wheeling this evening.

He glanced at the dash, then back on the pavement. "It's four o'clock. Wheeling's several hours from here. I don't want to interfere with your plans or anything, but why not stay in the cottage tonight and go back in the morning?"

If her situation weren't so dire, she would turn down his offer in a heartbeat. Olivia hated not having money. It was a precarious situation to be in. One with extremely limited options.

Tired from the long drive to Charity and from all the excitement of the day, Olivia struggled with what to do. The idea of staying in the cottage sure beat sleeping in her car. Or making the long drive back home—alone—in the dark. And it would be her new home for the next week or so.

Erik stopped in front of the big house and shut the engine off. "Call me old fashioned…" Erik broke through her thoughts. "But I can't stand the idea of you traveling alone at night. It would sure put my mind at ease if you'd stay. And if you're uncomfortable with staying at the guesthouse, I'll get you a hotel suite in town if that would make you feel better."

Was this man for real?

"Anyway, you haven't even seen your new house yet. By the time we finish dinner and I show you your new place, it'll be late. C'mon. What'd'ya say?"

Regardless of her situation, she found she couldn't say no to the hopefulness in his eyes. "I say yes." Relief slipped into her voice, but she didn't care.

"Good."

This must have been how Cinderella felt. Cinderella? Where had that come from? Olivia blew out a short breath. From watching one too many Cinderella movies growing up, that's where. Well, Olivia was no Cinderella. And, Prince Charming could just turn his steed's tail around and gallop the other way. She wanted nothing to do with any man ever again. Love wasn't like a fairy tale. Happily ever after? Nope. More like, fall in love, lose love, and suffer ever after.

Olivia forced her mind to still. She reached for the door handle but stopped when Erik swung her door open.

If ever there was a Prince Charming, she was certain he came in the form of Erik Cole. *Stop it, Olivia! He's your boss. Keep that fortress wall you've resurrected up. Don't you dare tear it down and leave yourself defenseless.*

Then Erik's hands splayed across her waist, and tingling molecules danced through her. A brick fell to the ground, leaving a gaping hole in her well-built stronghold.

Chapter Three

Four days after her interview with Erik, Olivia questioned the sanity of letting Haskell talk her into this. The only reason she finally caved in and agreed to go along with him was because the whole thing with Hammond still seemed surreal to her. Besides, she needed some kind of closure before starting her new life. "Are we almost there?" she asked, fighting to keep herself upright despite the bumps in the road.

"According to the map, it's right around this curve." Those words were the most they'd spoken to each other since leaving the airport. Neither one of them was dealing very well with what lay ahead of them.

While Haskell concentrated on keeping the SUV on the narrow road, Olivia studied his profile. Haskell's normally tanned face looked pale. He gripped the steering wheel so tight his knuckles were colorless.

They hit a pothole, jostling her in her seat. She braced herself and looked over at him. He kept his eyes fixed on the backwoods road. The pine and aspen trees lining the narrow man-made path made it difficult to stay out of the uneven tire grooves. If the vehicle jerked too far toward either side, they'd slam into a tree.

Olivia had never been claustrophobic, but the looming trees surrounding her smothered what little air she had.

At the top of the mountain trail, they rounded the

corner into a small clearing where several tree stumps dotted the ground, and huge stacks of stripped trees lay nestled against the forest.

Haskell stopped the vehicle and killed the engine.

She glanced over at him.

He sent her a tremulous smile, reached over and squeezed her hand, and then stepped out of the vehicle.

Outside, Olivia sucked in a sharp breath. Because of the bright sun and cloudless sky, she was unprepared for the dry, cold crispness of the Rocky Mountains. Born and raised in the northern panhandle of West Virginia, she'd only been to the Appalachian Mountains a few times. She had completely forgotten how high altitudes made for much cooler weather.

Knowing the unpleasant task ahead of her, her already jittery insides shook harder. Woodenly, she opened the back door of the SUV, dug in her backpack for the binoculars and a sweater, and slipped them on.

Haskell stood with his back to her. The slump in his shoulders ripped at her already frazzled heart. *I don't want to do this.* As if Haskell read her mind, he turned to her and reached out his hand. When Olivia placed her trembling palm in his, he sent her a sympathetic look.

His eyelids dropped, and his chest expanded. After a long sigh, he looked at her. "Ready?"

No! she wanted to shout. She'd never be ready. But rather than telling him that, she simply nodded.

One step behind Haskell, using his strength for balance, she focused on placing each foot securely on the uneven ground. Dry branches and brown pinecones crunched under her feet as she followed him to the edge of the steep mountainside. At the crest of the rocks, Haskell stopped, never looking at her. Instead, he kept his eyes forward. Forward to where Hammond's aircraft lay.

Before looking, Olivia closed her eyes, inhaling and exhaling several shaky breaths.

When she opened her eyes, her trail of vision slowly descended the steep canyon. Standing inches from the edge, the precipitous grade made her woozy. The idea of passing out and slipping into the river below made her shudder, so she braced her shoulder against Haskell's. Robotically he put his arm around her and pulled her tight against his side. Neither said a word.

Haskell turned glistening eyes toward her. A silent message passed between them as they clung to each other.

Not really wanting to, but knowing she had to see for herself if it really was Hammond's plane, she reached for the binoculars hanging around her neck and peered through them. With unsteady fingers she adjusted the knob.

The familiar plane came into view. "No," she whimpered, squeezing her eyes closed at the heart-wrenching sight. All remaining hope vanished. The binoculars dropped against her chest. Her vision swirled, and her numb body swayed. Haskell steadied her but didn't say a word. Olivia mentally thanked him for his silence because the last thing she wanted to do right now was talk.

Finally, she gathered up her nerve and looked through the binoculars again. Seeing Hammond's plane nestled on the side of the cliff, held in place only by a few pine trees, caused an eeriness to settle over her. The hair on her arms and neck rose. It looked as if someone had taken the aircraft and carefully wedged it into the trees, pressing it flat against the mountainside. It didn't even appear wrecked. How could that be?

She scanned the steep, rocky, tree-dotted ravine surrounding it and wondered if perhaps Hammond had survived, only to be lying in a hospital somewhere, not knowing who he was. When she took another glimpse at the plane and the steepness of the canyon, she knew that wasn't possible. Besides, someone would have contacted the authorities before now if he were.

As she continued to peruse the area, Olivia faced the fact that Hammond had probably died upon impact, and his body had either fallen into the ravine, or even worse, a bear or some other wild animal had dragged him off. At that revolting thought, her stomach lurched. She swallowed several times forcing the bitter acid back into her stomach.

Not able to handle one more second of being at the place where Hammond had suffered and another loved one had been ripped from her life, she pushed herself away from Haskell. "Take me home, please."

♥♥♥

Three days after her heartbreaking ordeal on the mountain, Olivia sighed with relief that she was leaving this dump of an apartment forever. The only thing squelching her joy was wondering what would happen if Hammond returned and….

Olivia shook her head. She had hoped that seeing his

plane would help her put the past to rest. But without a body, she still wondered if somehow he had survived. Her thoughts trailed to her parents. Again with the devastating déjà vu. As a young girl, she wondered if her parents had survived too. Nights upon lonely nights, she'd fantasized that her parents were lost on an island, waiting for some boat to bring them home. But that never happened. And she wasn't a child anymore. Just as she had finally accepted her parents' death, she needed to accept Hammond's and get on with her life. It sounded easy, but it would be one of the hardest things she ever had to do. But do it she must.

She snatched up her cat carrier, headed toward her car, and laid Samson on the front seat.

"Hello, Livvy."

Olivia whirled.

Her heart sank. So much for forgetting the past. She sighed. Why now? Up until the time they'd visited the plane crash site, Haskell had avoided her like an unwelcome disease. But now, the shoe was on the other foot. She wanted to avoid him. Every time she looked at Hammond's identical twin brother, memories of her missing fiancé washed over her afresh, breaking her heart all over again.

Knowing it wasn't Haskell's fault that the two of them looked and acted alike, she decided to be as friendly as she could without breaking down. "Hi, Haskell." She looked around the parking lot. "What are you doing here?"

Haskell peered at her loaded car. "You going somewhere?" His troubled gaze glanced between her and her vehicle.

Olivia closed her door and leaned against it. Drawing in a deep breath she looked at him and plunged forward. "Yes. I am. I need to make a clean break and start a new life for myself." She stared out at the parking lot and waved her hand in a wide arc. "Everywhere I look and everything I see reminds me of Hammond and what I've lost." She looked back at Haskell, defying him to argue with her.

"I understand." He sounded crushed.

Olivia pushed herself off of her car and laid her hand on Haskell's arm. His hand quickly covered hers as his pain-filled eyes raked over her face.

Forcing a lighter tone to her voice she squeezed his arm. "Take care, okay?"

His hand gripped hers. "Where ya moving to?"

As kindly as possible, she moved her hand out from under his and glanced at her watch. "Listen, I have to go."

Haskell gently grabbed her arm. "Don't go. Please, Livvy."

Pain and compassion treaded across her heart. While she felt sorry for him, she had to do what she had to do. Tenderly she removed his hand from her and looked into his eyes—eyes identical to Hammond's. Fresh pain ripped her heart. "I'm sorry, Haskell." With her gaze locked on his, she willed him to understand. "Every time I look at you, I see Hammond and the pain starts all over again." Tears slipped over her lids. "I can't handle this. I've got to go." With a quick jerk, she opened her car door, dropped herself behind the wheel, slammed the door, and started the engine.

To make sure she didn't run over Haskell, she peered

out the window. Something about the way Haskell's face matched the red in his shirt caused her to shudder. She quickly shoved her car into first gear. Without looking back, she drove away.

Still shaken over Haskell's reaction to her leaving, Olivia reached across the front seat and grabbed the cell phone her best friend Audra had given her as a going away present last night and pressed in her number.

"I'm on my way."

"I'm going to miss you." Audra's sad voice tugged at her heart. Well, the tiny bit that was left of her heart anyway.

"You're coming to visit me, right?"

"Just try and stop me."

"You won't believe what just happened." Olivia checked her side mirror before switching into the left lane. "Haskell showed up just as I was leaving. Whatever you do, don't tell him where I've moved to, okay?"

"I won't. And trust me, I totally understand. I'm just glad you're not leaving me behind too."

The torment of having to leave her best friend, the friend who saw her through some of the worst times of her life, completely disintegrated the few pieces of her heart that remained. "Never." She let the word emphasize her point for a moment. "Well, listen. I have to go. I'm about to get on the highway, and I need to pay attention to where I'm going so I don't get lost again."

"Okay. Keep in touch. Your cell phone service is paid up for a whole year, and you have unlimited long distance minutes."

"You didn't need to do that." Olivia's voice softened. "But thank you."

"You're welcome."

Olivia pulled up to the last traffic light before leaving Wheeling forever. "I'm gonna miss ya somethin' fierce, ya know?"

"Yeah, I know. Me too. Call me when you get there so I know you arrived safely, okay?"

"I will. Gotta go. I love you, Audra." As soon as the words left her mouth, she wanted to snatch them back. Everyone she loved died. She didn't want to love anyone ever again.

"I love you too."

Olivia recognized the pause and braced herself for the dreaded words that were coming next.

"Remember, Jesus loves you too."

"Yeah right," she muttered before ending her call.

The light turned green. Flipping a U-turn at the intersection, she headed toward the Riverfront one more time. She parked her car and stared at the place where she and Hammond used to set their lawn chairs. They had watched many a show on the big movie screen near the river's edge. Across the river, the reflection of trees and lights rippled in the water. The mountain silhouette in the background made such a romantic setting. Even though a sea of people had sat on the rows of concrete and patches of grass separating each row, it was as if she and Hammond were the only two people in the world. They shared many a kiss under the Riverfront's open sky.

Her thoughts traveled down the hallways of time. One

of her and Hammond's favorite things to do was the Winter Festival of Lights. They would drive over six miles through Oglebay Park to see the fantastic light show that covered more than three hundred acres. Among her favorites were, The Twelve Days of Christmas, the Candy Cane Wreath, The Willard Snowman, and the Snowflake Tunnel that hosted thousands of twinkling snowflakes.

As depression descended on her, Olivia realized she hadn't done all the things she'd planned to do before leaving Wheeling. At least one more time, she'd wanted to take the mile and half train ride at the Good Zoo, visit The Kruger Street Toy and Train Museum, watch the big boats come in and dock, see the laser show at the planetarium at Oglebay, and drive across the Wheeling Suspension Bridge that spanned the east channel of the Ohio river. But after coming to the Riverfront Movie sight and strolling down memory lane, she was glad she hadn't. Her already fragile soul wouldn't have been able to take it without completely falling apart.

Olivia wiped at the tears that trickled down her cheeks.

Scooting back in her seat, she engaged the clutch and started her car. Within minutes she was heading down the highway. She glanced over at her fifty-cent garage sale cat carrier. "Well, Samson. We're on our way to our new home."

Samson returned her comment with a nervous meow.

In a few hours, Olivia would be starting the job of her dreams and living in a house fit for a queen. A bit of her old adventurous spirit rose to the surface of her soul, and she did nothing to stop it.

Chapter Four

On his way to another monster truck rally, Erik kept thinking about Olivia, wondering how she'd gotten under his skin so quickly. Many a pretty woman had crossed his path, but none of them had affected him the way Olivia had. Why or how it happened he didn't know. But what he did know was she had.

So much so, that she even filled his dreams with her soft lips and her eyes the color of rich turquoise. He would gather her soft form into his arms and kiss her. Each time, she responded with a fervency that matched his own. And each time, before the mental picture took him to a place he refused to go, Erik had always awakened, praising God for putting an end to his dream. He quickly discovered it wasn't good for a man to dream about a woman he admired and was deeply attracted to. Especially when such passionate kissing was involved. He was *not* the type of man to think outside the box of marriage. His morals ran too deep for that. But, his chuckle reverberated inside the cab of his semi, he was still a man. A man who appreciated a woman's feminine curves and soft, husky voice... He forced his mind to not go there.

He pulled his semi into the contestant's area. His pit crew followed. Today, he'd be racing up against some of the best monster truck drivers in the world. His chances of winning were pretty slim, but he'd give it his best shot. After all, he'd never been one to back down from a challenge.

While Erik and his pit crew unloaded his two Mad Masher monster trucks and greeted the other drivers, Erik's mind kept straying toward Olivia. Man, he needed help. *You'd better get your act together before you race, bubba.*

♥♥♥

Erik was up next. From the middle of the seat in the Mad Masher, his heart ramped up to 1500 rpms when he got the green light. Hammer down all the way, he sped down thunder alley, slowed down at the hook, spun around and shoved the pedal to the floor. Up and over the ramp he leapt. The Mad Masher dead aired—landing on all four tires at once. The race over, Erik drove back to the pit and parked.

High fives made their way through his pit crew and some of his competitors. Second place was better than last.

Hours later, it was time for Erik to run the freestyle event.

Inside the arena, Erik drove the Mad Masher around a hook, then sped up as he headed toward a row of three vehicles. As he neared them, he let up on the gas then shoved his foot in to it just feet away from the first obstacle.

Iron-walling the first car, the Mad Masher flew

straight up, taking Erik's stomach with it.

Landing on its rear tires, still at an angle, his Chevy monster truck walked the van and the second car before resting on all fours.

Adrenaline raced through his veins as he powered his truck and headed straight toward his next target. Again he iron-walled the first car. On back wheels only, his truck walked the two, stacked cars, leapt upward at an angle, and cleared the moving van. His front tires connected first with the large storage container, and then his back wheels came down. Erik drove over the metal container and took a nosedive, before settling on all four wheels and bouncing. Erik rammed the pedal again, then slowed down before making another loop and then headed toward a row of six cars.

Up and over he flew, gaining a bit of air.

He hooked the Mad Masher again and headed toward another section of lined up vehicles. He iron-walled the first car, drove over the van, then a large school bus, another van and finally the last car. When his back tires landed, his truck bounced sideways, nearly flipping on its side. A quick ram to the gas pedal and the Mad Masher immediately straightened out.

Again, he swung around and leapt over a ramp. He ended up pogoing his truck. His pulse surged through him like a blower pushing fuel to the engine when the Mad Masher laid over on its side. Pieces shattered all over the place.

Safety officials were there in seconds to make sure he was okay. Erik released his harness and climbed up on the side of the Mad Masher, carefully making his way between the shattered pieces of his 1971 Chevy body. He stood, balancing himself between the two wheels. Then he raised his hands and gave major props to his fans. The crowd stood, roaring their approval.

What a rush! He lived for moments like these.

He, like all the drivers, deeply appreciated their fans. Without them, there would be no monster truck races.

While he got three nines and an eight for his efforts, his points couldn't touch John Seasock's score of three tens and a nine. The combination of John's expert driving and his Batman monster truck made him one dominating, powerful competitor. No wonder he was a two-time Monster Jam world finals champion.

After high fiving his competitors, Erik and his crew loaded up. The next day they headed for home with a second place in the racing event and a fourth place in the freestyle event. It had been a good weekend.

Ten days had passed since Erik had hired Olivia. On this bright, sunny Saturday, Olivia would move into his guesthouse. His heartbeat revved up at the thought of seeing her again.

"Don't you have something better to do?" Mickie Rhoads slapped Erik's hand as he ran it over the guest cottage windowsill. "I wiped everything down early this morning. You won't find a speck of dust anywhere."

Erik gave his housekeeper a repentant look. "I'm

sorry, Mickie. It's just that I want every thing to be perfect for Olivia. Something tells me she hasn't had an easy life, and I want to do everything in my power to change that."

"I would say you're already doing that by letting her live here."

He looked around the guesthouse and shrugged. "With all you have to do in here yet, will you have time to make dinner and have it ready when she arrives?"

Mickie planted her hands on her ample hips and sent him a glare. "Have I *ever* let you down?"

Erik held his hands up in surrender. "Okay, okay. I'm leaving now. I'll be back in…" He looked at his Chevy watch. "Three hours.""Thanks for the warning."

Erik laughed as he weaved his way through the furniture Mickie had shifted to the middle of the floor so she could vacuum.

Olivia would arrive in a few hours. He felt like a little kid on Christmas morning. Erik shook his head in amazement. He still couldn't get over how Olivia had gotten to him so quickly. Her pale turquoise-blue eyes never seemed far from his thoughts.

Back at Cole Chevrolet, Erik sat in his office, picked up a stack of papers, shuffled through them, dropped them onto his desk, and looked at his watch for the fiftieth time. Only five minutes had passed since the last time he'd checked. He ran his hand over his face and stared at the mountainous stack of papers. Again he questioned the sanity of his moving to West Virginia. *Be careful what you pray for*, his dad's words floated through his mind.

He'd prayed for a challenge, and God had answered him in spades. With some of the money he'd made from his sound investments, he'd purchased a Chevrolet dealership and renamed it Cole Chevrolet. However, he hadn't realized how much his family's combined effort kept everything running smoothly back home in Alabama. Here, it seemed there was always some catastrophe or another to deal with.

Erik glanced at the monster truck pictures on his walls. Olivia's idea for the Mad Masher popped into his head, and his mind immediately conjured up her turquoise eyes, her long crimped hair, and her soft full lips.

"Oh man. This is ridiculous. You just met the woman," he grumbled, rubbing the back of his neck. "I've got to get my mind off of her."

The stack of papers was as good a place as any to bury those thoughts, so he leaned forward and forced everything else from his mind. An hour later, the stack hadn't dwindled much. Every time he tried to concentrate on his work, his soon-to-be new neighbor invaded his thoughts. Too anxious to sit still, he jerked himself off of his chair and strode from the room. "Terri."

She looked up from her computer. "Yes, sir."

"I'm gonna be gone a couple of hours. If anyone calls, take a message."

"Will do." She turned and started typing.

Maybe a good workout at the gym would help him work off some of the anxiety.

An hour and forty-five minutes later, after some vigorous weightlifting and a long swim, Erik pulled into the driveway of his six hundred acre spread. According to Olivia's call and his calculations, he had just enough time to shower and clean up before her arrival. He took the stairs two at a time and carefully selected what he would wear. After showering, shaving, and splashing on some aftershave, he quickly slipped into his blue jeans, a light blue polo shirt, and his cowboy boots, then darted downstairs.

Gaze glued to the driveway, Erik stood back far enough from his front window so Olivia wouldn't see him waiting and watching for her.

Twenty minutes later, his heart kicked into overdrive when the familiar purple Nova turned up the driveway.

Not caring if he appeared anxious, he stepped out into the bright afternoon sun. As soon as she stopped, Erik was at her car door, opening it. "I see you made it okay." He couldn't keep his lips from tilting upward.

"Yes."

His smile slipped. *That was clever, Erik. You sounded like an idiot.*

She removed her sunglasses and placed them on her visor. With her hair pulled into a ponytail, she looked younger.

Erik extended his hand to help her. The moment their hands made contact, his brain cells stalled. That happened every time he was around her. *Get a grip, Erik.* He cleared his throat. "Would you like to come in and have something cold to drink?"

"That's really kind of you. But…" She looked up at him. Dark circles under her pale turquoise eyes tugged at his heart. "I'm really tired."

"Of course." He took a few steps back and looked around. "If you'd like to rest, I can keep an eye out for the movers."

"No need." Her cheeks turned pink. "Everything's in my car."

Her comment only reiterated what Erik had suspected. She was someone who was down on her luck. Well, not any more. Her luck was fixin' to change. He'd see to it personally.

A loud cat cry pierced the air, yanking Erik's attention from her to inside the car.

"That's Samson," she spoke through a yawn while patting her fingers against her lips. She walked around the front of her car, opened the passenger door, and pulled out a dilapidated cat carrier. On her way back toward him, she cooed to the animal.

Her gaze met his, and her smile vanished. "I forgot to ask if it was okay to bring my cat." Desperation filled those eyes that had haunted his sleep.

"Hey, not a problem." He did his best to give her a reassuring smile. "I have three cats myself."

Olivia set the carrier on top of her car. Tilting her head, she eyed him up and down. "I figured you more for the big watch dog type." Her sweet lips curled upward.

"Actually, I'm afraid of dogs."

Her heavy lashed eyes shot upward, and her mouth fell open.

Erik wanted to reach over and gently tap it shut.

Samson yowled again. Olivia's attention shifted back to her cat. "I'm sorry, but I need to unload my car so I can get his food and stuff. If you'll excuse me." She snatched up his carrier and sashayed the direction of the guesthouse.

"Wait." He pulled his gaze away from the gentle sway of her hips.

She stopped and turned back. "Yes?"

"Why don't you drive your car around back and park it in front of your house?"

Olivia's ponytail swayed back and forth. "Sheesh. I told you I was tired." As if to prove her point, another yawn escaped; this one wider and longer. Olivia covered her mouth with the back of her hand. "I just wanted to stop by and let you know I was here. But, I got distracted." She looked up at him and sent him that million dollar smile again.

Take it easy, man. Keep your wits about you.

"Sorry about that," he said. In two long strides he was in front of her and took the carrier. "I'll meet you around back." Without waiting for her answer he headed toward the cottage. Each step he took, his heart shifted into a higher gear. Hiring Olivia and bringing her to live near him was the best decision he'd ever made.

Olivia struggled against the fatigue overtaking her. Thanks to Erik's help, fifteen minutes later, all the boxes and worn out suitcases were out of her car and into her beautiful cottage. Relieved that he made no mention about her meager belongings, Olivia turned tired eyes up at him. “Thank you so much for all your help. And,” she looked around the cozy house, “for this.” Her gaze caught his. “I can’t thank you enough.”

“Hey, it’s like I said before. It’s you who’s helping me.” He rubbed his chin. “And Mickie.”

“Speaking of Mickie,” Olivia jumped in. “I hope she wasn’t too upset with you the other night. She made enough food to feed an entire orphanage. There was no way we could finish all that off.”

“Mickie loves to cook. And she loves to make sure that no one goes away hungry.”

Olivia laughed. “Well if anyone went away hungry that night, it wasn’t from a lack of food. I still can picture that huge bowl of coleslaw and platter of fried chicken.” She glanced up at him. The twinkle in her eyes made his smile broaden.

“You think that was impressive, you should see when my family comes for dinner.” He whistled.

“I can only imagine.” Olivia giggled. It was something she seemed to be doing a lot of since meeting Erik.

“Listen, I know you’re tired and you don’t want to join me for dinner, but would you mind if I brought food to you later?” His smile resembled that of a little boy who got caught with a frog in his pocket. “I hate to admit it, but I asked Mickie to fix something for tonight too. And well,” he shrugged, “you know how much food she makes and what will happen to me if it doesn’t get eaten.”

His playful actions and his rich masculine voice did

funny things to her insides. She found she couldn't say no to him. "That would be nice. Thank you. After all, we wouldn't want you to be in the dog house with your cook, now would we?" She smiled playfully.

Erik laughed and leaned back on the doorframe. "Hey, Mickie's more than just my cook. She keeps house for me too. You know how hard it is to find good help these days." He feigned a swoon.

No, she didn't know. A haze of sadness came over her as she looked at him. Before her parents had died, she lived in a middle class neighborhood and never wanted for anything. But she never knew this kind of wealth—the kind Erik was clearly used to.

"Well, listen," he said as he stepped back to her door and stopped. "I'll bring dinner around." He flipped his wrist and checked his watch. "Seven?"

Olivia nodded. "That would be great." She yawned again.

Erik chuckled. "See ya later. Get some rest." He opened her door and disappeared.

Olivia found Samson's litter box, filled it, and put it in the laundry room. Next, she filled her cat's bowl with food and water and then opened his carrier to let him out. Samson sniffed and cautiously raised one leg at a time as he checked out his new surroundings.

Knowing her cat was well taken care of, Olivia sprawled out on the nearest chair. Exhausted, she wondered why she ever agreed to let Erik bring her dinner. All she really wanted to do was go to bed and not wake up until Monday morning. Her body hung limp from all the stress she had endured the last couple of weeks—running out of money, the new job, the trip with Haskell and now moving.

By now, if it weren't for her getting this new job and beautiful home, she would have thought she was doomed to a jinxed life. But looking around her beautiful cottage she couldn't believe her luck.

Cottage didn't begin to describe her new home. Miniature mansion came to mind. Olivia couldn't believe it had four bedrooms. And each one had a different theme with rich, glorious colors. She chose the tropical island theme with its numerous brilliant shades of pinks, reds, purples, and yellow tropical plants, for her bedroom. Plus, it had an attached bathroom with a whirlpool bathtub.

A whirlpool bathtub!

Olivia pinched herself. Ouch. She definitely wasn't dreaming. All of this was real. Her sleepy gaze traveled around the living room. A half circle of floor to ceiling windows with a long, one piece white, light blue and navy scarf valance and sheer billowy voile panels gave the living room a light airy look.

The large palm tree that separated the windows and the French doors leading to an open patio reminded her of the last vacation she'd taken with her parents. They'd gone to Florida and had a great time. Then one month later they were gone. Sadness tried to weave its spell over Olivia, but she forced her mind back on to more pleasant things.

She couldn't wait to light the gas fireplace and run her fingers over the smooth navy blue marble. Marble? Who would have thought that she, Olivia Roseman, would ever live in such luxury? No longer able to keep her eyes open,

Olivia drifted off to sleep.

Hours later, a ringing doorbell brought Olivia's eyelids flying open, and her gaze darted about the room before she figured out where she was. Moving Samson off her chest, she slid her feet to the plush floor. "Just a minute," she hollered through a sleep-induced yawn.

Olivia swaggered across the room and opened the door.

"Delivery." Erik smiled and held up a wicker basket. For a split second, the white of his eyes showed, and then returned to normal. "I didn't wake you, did I?"

Olivia patted down her hair. "You did. But that's fine."

"Oh. I can come back later if you'd like."

"No, it's fine. Really. C'mon in." Olivia moved sideways to let him in, stifling a lingering yawn.

When he walked by, a spicy aroma teased her senses and made her stomach growl noisily. Certain that red stained her cheeks, she turned toward her cat. "Samson! Really!" she playfully chastened him. The gray, longhaired tomcat raised his eyes as if to inquire what her problem was. "Now don't you be snarling at this nice man." She picked him up and held him out in front of her. He hung limp as a piece of yarn. "Shame on you." Gold, unfazed eyes stared back at her. Olivia tucked him to her chest. "You naughty kitty." Her fingers rubbed the back of his neck.

"I'm shocked." Erik turned to her with a droop of a frown. "How could you blame that poor defenseless cat for your stomach noises?"

Olivia feigned shock. “Me? Why, I would never do something like that.” She laughed, and Erik joined her.

Olivia couldn’t believe how relaxed she felt around her new boss. But then again, he had a way of putting her at ease.

She cuddled her cat to her chest. “I’m sorry, Sammy. I shouldn’t have blamed you. Can you forgive me?”

Samson’s motor started.

“There.” She glanced at Erik. “Satisfied?”

Erik planted his free palm against his chest and nodded. “Muuuccch better.”

They both smiled. Olivia glanced at the basket. “Oh.” She put Samson down. “I’m sorry. I don’t know where my manners are. Let me take that.” She extended her hand toward him.

He moved it from her grasp. “That’s okay. I’ve got it. Where would you like me to put it?”

She moved a box out of his way and headed toward the kitchen. “Follow me.”

On the way to the dining area, she snagged a glimpse of herself in a mirrored picture and nearly tripped from the shock. Her hair scrunchee must have fallen out while she slept. In seconds, she corralled her wild tresses, twisted them in one long piece, and tossed it over her shoulder. No wonder the whites of Erik’s eyes showed when she opened the door. She looked a fright. She giggled at the thought and then reprimanded herself for acting like a love-struck teenager.

“What’s so funny?” Erik asked as he followed her through the rooms.

Olivia kept walking and mouthed the word oops. She hadn't realized she had laughed out loud.

She stopped, and faced him. "I was thinking about my hair and how it looked when I answered the door." Not wanting to see his response, she whirled, and finished the few steps into the dining area. Then she glanced out the sliding glass window and saw how beautiful it looked outside. "Do you mind if we sit outside on the patio chairs?"

Pleasure splayed across his face. "Don't mind at all. Lead the way."

Olivia reached for the door handle just as Erik's hand landed on top of hers.

Their gazes locked for the briefest of moments before Olivia removed her hand and allowed him to open the door.

She stepped out into the warm evening and breathed deeply the scent of lush foliage and soil.

They sat down and filled their plates. Erik bowed his head. Olivia didn't. Instead, she stared at the man sitting across from her. The man whose kindness had given her a reason to get up in the mornings again. The man who made her feel less lonely and actually made her laugh again. The man who, if she wasn't careful, could be very dangerous to her well being.

Chapter Five

Erik forced his mind back to the task at hand. He thumbed through the small stack of paperwork he needed to finish. People were waiting on him to approve their automobile offers. He ran over the figures of one offer, but his mind refused to focus on it. His thoughts kept wheeling backward to a certain little beauty.

Sitting with Olivia, sharing a meal was as natural as breathing. Her sweetness captivated him. He really wanted to get to know her better. The day Olivia had arrived, Mickie and her husband Virgil had stopped by to welcome her. Olivia had invited the middle-aged couple to join them and won their hearts with her thoughtfulness. She seemed more relaxed with them around. It was as if she didn't really want to be alone with him.

In fact, she spent more time talking to Mickie and Virgil than she did him. But, it hadn't really bothered him because he liked sitting back, watching the way her eyes lit up whenever she talked about how much she loved the challenge of designing a perfect fit for her customers, of the finer techniques of airbrush painting and the exciting process from beginning to end, and of the pleasure of seeing the customers' beaming faces at the finished product. One thing was for sure, she was passionate about her work. But not about family.

Whenever any of them asked Olivia about her family

or her parents, sadness blinked through her eyes, and she immediately either avoided the subject or changed it.

He wondered why.

He also wondered what she was doing now.

A glance at the collector series car clock on his office wall showed 10:48. If he hurried, he'd have time to grab some food and head out to his place and share lunch with her.

Like a cyclone, he whizzed through the offers, signing the ones he approved and proposing counter offers to the others.

Another darting gaze at the Chevelle clock, and he jumped up. 11:36. He gathered the offer approvals and headed out his office door.

"Here, Terri." He laid them on her desk. "I'm going to lunch. I'll be back in a couple of hours."

"Couple of hours, huh?"

Erik frowned at the mirth in her voice and eyes. "Terri," he drew out in warning.

Terri raised her hand in defense. "What?" The innocent look she gave him didn't fool him one little bit.

"You know what." He tried to keep his tone firm, but his secretary knew him too well. "Yes. I'm going to have lunch with Olivia. And yes, I like her." He wagged his finger at her. "But don't you go readin' anymore into this than there is."

"Me?" She pressed her fingertips against her chest. "Would I do that?"

"Yeah. You would. I gotta run. See ya later." Erik left the building and trotted toward his truck.

The drive to his place had never seemed so long. He couldn't wait to see Olivia again. This was her first day on the job, and he couldn't wait to watch her work. Truthfully, he could watch her watch paint dry and it would be completely fascinating to him.

He pulled his truck up to the shop, threw it in park, and shut it off. After he got out, he reached for the bag of food and headed toward the shop door.

Inside, upbeat music filled the building. Olivia stood by the door of the Mad Masher. One arm lay across her stomach, the other tilted upward, supporting her fingers as they tapped her lips. Her loose-fitting, faded blue jeans and baggy red T-shirt hid her feminine figure. Some kind of fancy braid bound her long hair together. Tied in a knot at the back of her head, peeking from under her bangs, was a blue, red, and white bandanna. Steel-toed-boots covered her feet. What a different sight from the day she'd walked into his office. Professional businesswoman attire didn't suit her. Or him. Truth be known, he liked this image much better.

"Hi, there." Erik greeted her cheerfully as he closed the door behind him.

Olivia's hand flew from her lips as she spun around and splayed her hand near the base of her neck. "Lands o' Goshen! You scared the liver out of me."

"So I noticed." He chuckled, walking closer to her. "Lands o' Goshen, huh? Where'd that come from?"

She turned back to the truck. "My Mimi, who was born in Arkansas and grew up in Texas. She said it all the time, and I picked it up." She shrugged, her gaze already back on the door of the monster truck.

"I see. You sure looked like you were in deep thought." He stopped at her side.

"I was." She glanced at him then back at the truck.

"A penny for your thoughts?"

Those turquoise eyes looked up at him. "Keep your penny. It's not worth it." She grinned. "I was planning the image I want to paint on the door and deciding what I want to do first."

"You're right. That wasn't worth a penny." Her gaze flew to his. "Gotcha." He chuckled. "It would have been worth more than a penny to me. But, hey, your loss." He held up his hand. "You passed on the penny."

"You're impossible. You know that?"

"That's what Camara tells me."

"Camara?" She tipped her head.

"My little sister."

"Oh. Her name is Camara? Like in Camaro?"

"Yeppers."

She nodded. "It's definitely unique. I like it."

"Her full name is Camara Chevelle Cole."

Surprise transformed Olivia's face, making her even cuter. "Camara Chevelle Cole, huh?"

"Well, make that Lamar. She's married now."

"So," Olivia tilted her head and pursed her lips to the side. "What middle name did your parents give you?"

"They named him after our grandfather. Erik Mannory Cole." His aunt's voice hijacked his attention.

Erik pivoted toward the door. "Aunt Adell!" In a few steps, he was by his aunt's side, hugging her. "What are you doing here?"

♥♥♥

Olivia's hand flew to her head. She patted her hair before remembering that she'd braided it. Still, her attire wouldn't make for a great first impression. She looked down at her jeans and pulled at her T-shirt, wishing a fairy godmother could get her out of this one.

"I came by to meet and welcome your new neighbor." His aunt brushed past him and scuttled over toward her. Olivia swallowed hard and swiped her sweaty palms down the front of her pants.

Erik quickly stepped up beside his aunt who was dressed in a bright pink tailored pantsuit with matching shoes. Her vibrant radiance flooded the room with sunshine and happiness. "Olivia. This is my aunt, Mrs. Preston. My mother's sister."

"Oh tootles." His aunt gave him a pat on his arm. "Forget this Mrs. Preston business. My name is Adell." She extended her hand toward Olivia and shook it. "Mrs. Preston makes me sound way too old." The laughing crinkles around the woman's eyes reminded Olivia of her mother's. Olivia shook off the sad thought, along with the other string of emotions that accompanied it every time she thought about her mother, and forced a smile onto her face. "Nice to meet you, Mrs.—Adell."

Genetics had been good to the tiny lady standing in front of her. Perfectly shaped, dusty rose lips curled into a sweet smile, revealing even white teeth. Several silver strands mingled throughout her blonde flip style hair-do. Erik definitely got his gorgeous brown eyes and handsome features from his mother's side of the family.

"Nice to meet you too. I've heard so many wonderful things about you."

Olivia darted a curious gaze toward Erik, who looked sheepish.

"I told Aunt Adell how talented you are. And how amazing your art work is."

"I see." Relief sprouted over her when she realized he didn't know anything else about her or her past.

"Well, listen. I won't keep you. I just wanted to give you this." His aunt handed her a large cloth-covered basket that jerked Olivia's arm down with its weight. "And to welcome you to Charity, Olivia." Adell hugged her before turning toward her nephew.

Olivia hugged her biceps. His aunt's embrace, although brief, made her lonesome for more. Many nights, long, long ago, when something frightened Olivia, or she needed comforting for whatever reason, her mother would wrap her in her arms and tell her a story. Sometimes a Bible story, sometimes a made up story, or sometimes it would be a story about when her mother grew up. Whatever it was, it was always comforting and uplifting. Somehow this woman's hug had the same effect on her.

"You'll come, won't you?"

Olivia blinked. *Come? Come where?* Olivia's mind scrambled to figure out what Adell was talking about. She should have never allowed her thoughts to travel down the passageway of time. That always got her into trouble.

"You can ride with Erik." Adell nodded at Erik, obviously seeking his approval.

Ride with Erik? Ride with Erik where? Her gaze traveled between Erik and his aunt.

"Definitely." He smiled at Olivia.

"Good. It's settled then."

Settled? What's settled? Olivia hoped one of them would say something that would clue her in to what was going on. Now would be a great time for a piece of gum. If there was ever a time she needed calming, now was it. Just what exactly had she gotten herself into this time?

"Five o'clock work for you?" Adell asked Olivia.

Work for me? Work for me for what? Well, whatever it was, she would agree and then afterwards she would slap herself for not paying attention. "Five's fine."

"Great. See ya then." As fast as his aunt had appeared, she disappeared. That seemed to happen a lot around here. People blew in and out of places like a tornado. They were here one minute and gone the next.

"That's so awesome," Erik said. "I'm so glad you're able to make it. You'll get to meet everyone there."

There? Lands o' Goshen! Olivia knew she'd better find out just what she was doing and when. She opened her mouth to ask, but Erik said, "My aunt lives for parties. Your being a newcomer here just gives her another excuse to throw one. Aunt Adell will invite our whole church congregation and all the neighbors within miles. She'll have enough hickory smoked pork with barbeque sauce, fried trout, fried catfish, fried chicken, deep fried cheese grit balls, fried apples, homemade bread, apple butter, and who knows what else, to feed an entire town." He patted his stomach. "She's worse than Mickie. No one goes away hungry that's for sure."

Wait. Was his aunt throwing this party for her? Embarrassed that she hadn't been paying attention, Olivia didn't dare ask. "I'm looking forward to it. When is it again?"

"Three weeks from now on Sunday. It takes her weeks to prepare."

A thread of panic wound its way around Olivia's throat, threatening to suffocate her. Her mind rummaged through her scarce closet. Was this a casual affair or a formal affair? Whatever it was, her wardrobe wouldn't be sufficient. Her only nice outfit, she'd worn to her job interview. Not knowing when payday was, she wasn't sure she'd have money or time to go shopping before then.

"Are you okay?" Erik stared at her in that way that short-circuited her brain.

Olivia forced her lips upward. "I'm fine. I was just trying to figure out what to wear." Her eyes widened. She couldn't believe she'd just told her boss that she was trying to figure out what to wear. *What an idiot.* She could feel a blush coming on.

"Well, whatever ya do, don't wear anything fancy. Aunt Adell doesn't want anyone's clothes soiled from all that greasy, messy food. She says those little plastic bibs are about worthless because they barely catch the mess. Besides, if our clothes don't get dirty while eating, they do when we play games."

The thought of food made her stomach growl.

Erik chuckled. “You have the loudest stomach of anyone I’ve ever met.”

“My mother did—” Olivia stopped herself.

He tilted his head inquisitively. “Your mother did what?”

Olivia mashed down the melancholy that threatened to rise up. “My mother’s stomach growled loud too. Dad used to tease us about it all the time. He said one loud growling stomach was enough to alert the neighborhood, but two, alerted the whole town to the fact that the Roseman women were hungry.” Olivia smiled softly at the memory. It was one among a thousand she’d forgotten since the accident.

“Do your parents live in Wheeling?”

Not wanting to talk about her parents or their deaths, Olivia jerked her wrist around. “Well, will you look at the time?” She refused to respond or even acknowledge the strange look on Erik’s face. “If I don’t get back to work my boss is going to fire me.” She walked over to the bench and picked up a Srathmore Bristol board so she could get started on her preliminary mock up.

Erik followed her. Reaching out, he barely touched her arm. “Hey, we haven’t even eaten yet. Trust me. I know your boss. He won’t fire you. You’re the best thing that’s happened to him since fresh baked apple pie.”

The statement twined through her in ways she didn’t want to admit. What did he mean by the best thing that had happened to him? Hammond had said something similar to her the day before he had disappeared. Her heart cried afresh. Would she ever forget him or her past?

Chapter Six

Had he said something wrong to cause their easy bantering to vanish? While he sat outside the shop on the picnic table situated under the large oak tree, Erik foraged through his brain, seeking the answer to his silent question even as his hand rummaged in the bag for a packet of salt. The last words he'd spoken to Olivia were something about her being the best thing since fresh baked pie. Was that out of line? Maybe he shouldn't have been that honest.

Erik studied Olivia as she removed the upper part of her cheeseburger bun and placed it on the sandwich wrapper. Head bowed, she nibbled on her sandwich and avoided looking at him. Her wariness and nervousness tore at his heart. Not once did she look up at him. Something was wrong, and he wanted to know what it was. After much deliberation, he decided there was no sense in not asking. "Olivia." He kept his voice soft as he tore open the packet of salt and sprinkled it on his French fries.

Her eyes slowly connected with his.

"Are you okay?" It seemed as if he was constantly asking her that question.

Her gaze fell to her burger. "I'm fine." The sadness in her voice did nothing to reassure him.

"Did I say something to offend you?"

Once again she looked up at him. "No."

That answer and tone didn't help. "Was I too presumptuous in bringing you lunch?"

"No, no." She waved her hand barely looking at him. "It was very sweet of you to bring me lunch. I'm sorry. I was just—" She placed her cheeseburger on the picnic table, picked up her bottled Coke, and took a drink. Her gaze transferred to somewhere off in the distance.

Erik watched her for several moments, waiting for her response. He picked up a cold French fry, popped it into his mouth and chewed slowly, hoping that would give her the space to start. The pain in her eyes said that whatever bothered her went way deep.

A female cardinal hopped its way over to them. Erik picked up a French fry and tossed it to the brown bird, tinged with red on its crest, wings, and tail. It chirped its thanks, snatched it up, and flew away.

Within seconds a male cardinal with its bright red crest, black face, and stout red bill swooped down. The bird's loud *what-cheer-cheer-cheer* snagged Olivia's attention. She tore off a piece of bread and tossed it to the bird. The bird flew a couple of yards away, then cautiously trotted back to the morsel. It pecked at the bread. While eating that bite, another bird swooped down and joined it. The second bird, a much more aggressive cardinal, stole the piece she'd thrown. Olivia laughed as the first bird looked up in stunned puzzlement.

Erik's gaze swung to her. She quickly tore off another piece and tossed it toward the incredulous bird. It hopped to the bread, and this time it snatched up the other piece when another bird headed toward it chirping *what-cheer-cheer-*

cheer so loudly that Erik wanted to cover his ears.

Olivia bent her neck back and gazed high into the tree branches above them. “I didn’t even know there were any birds in this tree when we sat down.” Joy lit her face. “But boy, once that first one showed up, now there’s a small flock gathering.” She giggled as she watched the birds fighting over the French fry he’d just tossed.

Whatever happened earlier to make her so sad had disappeared like the fried potato stick they’d fed to the birds.

“They’ll stay here as long as someone feeds them.”

She looked at him and then went back to her hamburger although she more picked at it than ate it. “Do you feed them often?”

Erik tossed another fry and leaned his elbows on the table. “On Saturdays mostly. Whenever I work on the Mad Masher, I eat out here. In fact...” He stood and grabbed his French fries. The birds flew back into the tree. Erik lowered himself onto the grass and patted the spot next to him.

Puzzled but curious, Olivia slid off the bench and parked herself beside him, but not too closely.

He extended a French fry toward her.

She tilted her head and looked at him.

He reached over and turned her palm upward. Ignoring the tremor shimming up his arm, Erik placed the fry in her hand. “Hold your palm flat on the ground, and one of the birds will come and eat right out of your hand.”

Olivia jerked her hand back, clutching it to her chest. “No, that’s okay.”

Was that fear in her eyes? Where had the joy from a few minutes ago gone? Erik turned his body to face her. "Are you okay?"

"There's those words again." Her nervous smile made him want to wrap her in his arms and make whatever had her so fearful and fidgety disappear. "It's just that—"

When she looked away from him, Erik couldn't help himself. "It's just what?" he asked, purposely keeping his tone soft. Whatever was bothering her, he wanted her to know she could trust him because the one thing that rose up in his spirit repeatedly was Olivia needed a friend.

She looked back at him, and Erik saw the question in her eyes. "Whatever is bothering you, Olivia, you can trust me."

A quick frown took over her features before they returned to normal. She drew in a deep breath. "When I was growing up, my—" she paused as her gaze slid out to the day around them. "One of my chores was to feed the parrot. But this parrot wasn't friendly. Every time I fed it, it bit me." As if in a fog, she looked at her hands. "His beak was razor sharp."

Erik followed her gaze. Thread thin scars covered her forefingers and thumbs, and anger rose in him. What kind of parent kept a bird that attacked a child?

Her gaze returned to his. "I don't mind feeding birds from a distance, but there's no way I want one to come near me."

What do I do here, Lord?

Don't say anything. Just show her it's okay to feed them.

Erik pulled a French fry out of its paper sleeve and laid the fry in the palm of his hand before lowering it onto the grass. He watched her, watching his hand.

Within seconds one of the cardinals swooped onto the grass and skipped its way over to Erik. The bird hopped onto Erik's hand and pecked at the French fry. Once it had eaten a couple of bites, it snatched up the rest, and flew off.

Uncertainty and anxiousness flitted across Olivia's face.

He repeated the process a few more times. Each time Olivia looked surprised, and her taut shoulders loosened with each snatched up morsel.

"Ya wanna try it?" Erik asked softly.

Olivia trained her wide-eyed gaze on him.

"It's okay," he whispered. "Trust me. He won't hurt you."

Finally she nodded, and Erik handed her a fry.

Her attention went back toward the bird. She laid her hand flat on the ground. Each step the bird took closer to her, Olivia yanked her stiff neck backward another notch. The bird hopped onto her hand, and a small gasp escaped Olivia. The bird leapt back, then cautiously came toward her again. This time when it hopped onto her palm, Olivia stayed stock-still. Her attention never swayed from the bird. Was it due to fear that if she looked away the bird might attack her like the parrot had, or was it fascination? He hoped it was the latter, but he refused to ask and risk breaking the enchantment of the moment.

A quick peck and it held a small piece in its beak. Soon another bird came, chased off the other one, and hopped onto Olivia's palm. It, too, took a piece, then fluttered away. In the blink of an eye, another bird landed on her palm and snatched the last of the fry.

When it was gone, Olivia relaxed. She turned and looked at him. A slight curl lifted the corners of her mouth. One thought came to his mind—childlike innocence.

Neither spoke as he one-by-one handed her the fries until they were all gone, then he stood and helped her up.

"Wow. That was amazing." She sighed deeply before looking at him. "Thank you. That was so fun." She glanced at her watch. "Oh, I'm sorry." The guilt on her face was so cute. "It's nearly one thirty." She quickly gathered up their trash. "I'll work late tonight to make up for it."

"Olivia." He softly laid his hand on top of hers to still her skittering. "It's okay. I know the boss. And he doesn't mind." He smiled and winked at her. "And you don't have to work late. After all, I'm the one who brought you out here and got ya ta feedin' the birds. So, if anyone should have to work late, it should be me."

He picked up his Coke and downed the rest. "Thanks for having lunch with me."

"No, thank you. That was so sweet of you to bring me lunch." She glanced toward the lawn where the birds hung several yards back. About five of them still skipped over the grass, stopping to peck at something every so often. "I know where I'll be eating my noon meals from now on." She transferred her focus on to him and smiled. "Well, I'd better to get back to work. I wouldn't want to get fired the first day on the job." With that she finished gathering the trash and jogged toward the shop, hollering over her shoulder. "Thanks again, Erik."

"Anytime," he whispered. "Anytime."

♥ ♥ ♥

Olivia stepped into the air-conditioned shop and dropped the trash into the barrel right inside the door. She shut the door and leaned against it. That was the nicest lunch she'd had in a long time. Not once had she thought of Hammond throughout the meal.

Hammond, she sighed.

The door swung open, throwing Olivia forward. She scrambled to regain her balance but couldn't. Her knees and hands slammed against the concrete floor.

"Olivia!" Erik quickly knelt before her. "I'm sorry. I didn't know you were there."

Olivia twisted her body around, sat on her backside, and folded her knees against her chest, wrapping her arms around her legs. Her hands and knees stung.

"Are you okay?"

She forced a smile to her lips. "Do you notice how often you say those words to me?" Bypassing the pain, she forced lightheartedness into her tone, and grinned.

Erik didn't return her smile. Concern flooded through his eyes. "I'm so sorry."

Olivia shifted her hands behind her back and started to push herself up. Quicker than a heartbeat, Erik leapt up and helped her to her feet. A warm sensation flowed through her arm, surprising her with its intensity. She gazed up at him briefly, then shrugged from his grasp. "Thank you."

She brushed the back of her pants and knees off.

"Are you sure you're okay?" His concern was duly noted, and she appreciated it even though there was no need for it. After all, no real harm had come to her. And besides, how was he supposed to know she was leaning against the door? The need to put his mind at ease pressed into her.

"I'm just fine. Really." She sent him a reassuring smile. "That's what I get for sloughing off. I should have gotten right back to work and none of this would have happened." She laughed, hoping to make him feel better. But her effort failed. He didn't even crack a smile. Not knowing what else to do to erase the worry from his handsome face, she finally asked, "Did you need something?"

His forehead creased with confusion. "What?"

"Did you forget something?"

He stared at her for a moment. Obviously, still upset about knocking her to the floor, it took a minute before dawning lit his features. "Oh, yeah." He nodded. "I almost forgot to ask if you wanted to come to my house for dinner."

"Dinner?" He wanted to have dinner with her? Her eyelashes connected numerous times.

"Yeah, as in," he held his hand in the air, dipped it, and brought it to his mouth as if he was eating, "you know, dinner." He smiled.

Olivia pondered his invitation. Maybe she shouldn't eat so many meals with her boss. It was sure to invite ideas that she didn't want any part of. Sure, he was trying to be neighborly and all, but she didn't want anything to jeopardize her job. As much as she enjoyed his company, she decided to put an end to the invitations.

"Thanks. But I have plans." It wasn't a lie. She had planned to open a package of Ramen noodles and then take a swim. After all, Erik told her she could use the pool and facilities here whenever she wanted.

"Oh."

At the sound of his disappointment, Olivia's attention flew to Erik's.

His broad chest heaved, and he released a weighty sigh. "Well, while you're doing whatever it is you're doing, don't worry about me. It's okay. Really. I can face Mickie's wrath all by myself." He dragged out the word 'all' and sighed again. Only this time his sigh had a much more dramatic flare to it. That, and the mirth in his eyes, caused the laughter to bubble up and spring out of her like an unexpected geyser.

"Well, I guess we can't have that now, can we?" Why was it so hard to just tell him no? Olivia didn't know why, but she found she couldn't turn him down no matter how good her intentions were. "Okay, I'll change my plans. What time?"

"Six-thirty." He stepped closer. "Listen, I don't want you to feel manipulated into coming to dinner. I was just teasing about Mickie. The woman loves to give me a hard time." Erik rubbed his chin. "I just thought with you being new here and all that you might want to spend some time with a friend."

Friend? Is that what they were? Was it safe to have her

boss as her friend? More to the point was it safe to have *this* boss as her friend?

♥♥♥

Thursday morning brought with it heavy overcast skies and thunderous rain. Storms like this used to bother Olivia. They always reminded her of the cloud of doom that seemed to hover over her life. But that was changing. Everyone here in Charity had been so nice to her.

Several neighbors had stopped by to welcome her and even brought her gift baskets laden with snacks, fruit, crackers, cheese, a variety of bagels, cookies, nuts, chocolates, coffee, and a tin of different flavored teas. Some brought her casserole dishes and salad fixings. Along with the abundance of food Erik had stocked in her refrigerator, freezer, and cupboards when she first arrived, she now had enough food to last her a couple of months or more. Olivia couldn't stop her lips from turning upward. It was so nice to not be hungry or to have to eat Ramen noodles every day. Not that she didn't like Ramen noodles, she did. She loved them. But just not every day for months on end.

After she drank her Red Raspberry Zinger tea and ate her toasted raisin bagel smeared with butter, Olivia grabbed the windbreaker Audra had given her for Christmas last year, and headed out the door toward the shop.

She stepped inside the massive building, shook off her wet jacket, and hung it on a hook. With three monster truck bodies to finish, she got right to work.

Late yesterday afternoon, she had finished painting all three fiberglass bodies in a medium shade of blue. While they were drying, she had reassessed her canvas—the monster truck—and had made a few changes to the mock up drawing she'd done in pencil. Then she had drawn a preliminary color mock up using a Strathmore illustration board. Her favorite brand.

Today, she hoped to transfer the picture onto the doors, using grease pencils and a projector. She pressed her hand over the length of her face. Lands o' Goshen, she still had a lot to do.

Good thing Erik's next monster truck race wasn't until next weekend, and that he'd told her not to worry about getting them done by then because he would use the same fiberglass bodies he'd been using. She sighed with relief because she still had to mask the areas with Frisket film and masking tape and airbrush in a rough up on the truck. Plus, the most time consuming part was yet to come—gradually adding in the detail work.

And finally, she would apply several coats of clear coat paint. That was the most arduous and the most rewarding part. Roughing up each layer with sandpaper, so that the next layer of lacquer had something to stick to, was the arduous part. Applying the final layer of clear coat was the rewarding part. Well, that, and being able to stand back and admire the deeper, and slightly darker, creative masterpiece. Artwork was something she absolutely loved doing. And speaking of, she'd better get back to it. With any luck at all, she'd have at least one of the trucks done by next week.

She heard the shop door open. Without looking she already knew who it was. Every morning Erik stopped by before heading out to work.

"Good morning, Erik."

"Sorry to disappoint you, but I'm not Erik."

Her neck stiffened. Olivia closed her eyes and willed a tolerant attitude into herself. She was going to need it. She eased around and forced a smile onto her face. "Morning, Ben."

The last three mornings, Ben Hobbs had stopped by on his way to the pit crew shop next door. Each time he did, it was minutes after Erik left. Something about that made her uneasy. Why, she didn't know. Ben seemed like a nice enough guy even though he strutted around like a proud rooster. His light green eyes and dark brown hair were an attractive combination. But he didn't tempt her. Besides, there was something about him that... That what? Reminded her of Markus? Her spine scrunched up and down at that thought.

Only a mere three feet separated them now. Feeling claustrophobic by his nearness, she stepped back. He stepped closer.

Her brain scrambled for a solution. Knowing she had lots to do, she got right to the point. "Is there something I can do for you?" As soon as the question left her lips, Olivia wanted to snatch it back.

A gleam sparked through his eyes. "No, I'm just being friendly."

Yeah, she just bet he was.

"I figured with you being new to the neighborhood and

all that you'd like some company." Again with the gleam in his eyes.

Not yours. She wished he'd just go away and leave her alone.

"Olivia, I wondered if…"

Olivia's attention shot to the door as Ben whirled.

Erik looked at her and then at Ben. "Morning, Ben." He headed toward him.

"Morning, boss." Ben took a full step backward.

Again Erik's gaze vacillated between her and Ben.

Ben faced her although he was visibly nervous now. "Well, I'd better get to work or the boss here," he jerked his head toward Erik, "might fire me." An uncertain smile crooked his mouth.

"You got that right," Erik joked, but the joke didn't quite meet his eyes. Ben must have noticed it too because he quickly worked his way to the door.

"See ya later, Olivia." With that he slipped outside. And boy was she ever relieved that he did.

♥♥♥

Erik watched Ben leave. He wondered what the man was up to and if there was something going on between him and Olivia. When he stopped by the mechanics shop to talk to Ben, Ted told him that Ben was probably at the paint shop again. Erik didn't even wait for an explanation. He rushed right over here.

He locked eyes with Olivia. Was it just his imagination or did she seem more relaxed than she had when he first walked in?

"Is Ben bothering you?"

Olivia's eyelids lowered. "Not really."

"Not really as in 'Yes, he is,' or not really as in 'No, he isn't'?"

♥♥♥

What should she say? Olivia didn't want to cause any trouble, but something about Ben gave her the willies. While she mulled over how to answer him, Erik stepped closer. "I can see he makes you uncomfortable. I'll talk to him."

Her wide eyes blasted upward. Fear snaked around her spine. If Erik said something to him, would it make matters worse?

"Hello." Adell's chipper voice shattered her thoughts.

Today must be Olivia's day for visitors.

"Hi, nephew." Adell floated toward them. She stopped long enough to give Erik a brief hug before pulling Olivia into her arms. This woman was quick. "Hi, Miss Olivia. I stopped by to see if you'd like to have lunch with me today." Adell glanced over at Erik. "You can come too if you'd like."

The bubbling, bouncy woman manufactured enough energy to create a small whirlwind, and happiness emanated from her. Olivia envied Erik having such a sweet person like Adell for an aunt.

"Well, what do you say?" Adell's stiff flip hairdo didn't budge when she whipped her head back and forth between her and Erik.

"You name the time, Auntie, and we'll be there." He glanced at Olivia looking for her approval.

She gave a quick nod. "Sounds like fun." Olivia was surprised that she actually meant it.

"Great." Adell pressed her palms together. "I'll meet you both back here at noon." Darting a quick glance at the 1971 Chevy fiberglass molds, she pointed her finger toward the monster trucks. "I love that shade of blue," she tossed out, then out the door she flew before either of them had a chance to comment or respond.

Side by side Olivia and Erik stood, staring at the door. Dumbfounded, they slowly looked at each other.

"I guess this means we're going to lunch," he said through a chuckle. And what a nice chuckle it was.

"I guess you're right." In the last four days, Olivia had entertained more company than she had in years. Everyone had gone out of their way to make her feel welcome. Cared for and loved even.

Loved.

The one thing she greatly feared. Would she ever be free to love again? Would she ever want to love again?

Chapter Seven

For two weeks she'd lived in the beautiful house. Looking around, Olivia marveled at how different life could be when she didn't have to worry about money or where her next meal was coming from.

Olivia settled herself onto the comfy blue couch in the cottage and hummed while dialing Audra's number. It was completely unbelievable how happy she had become in such a short time.

"Hello."

"Hi, girlfriend. Are ya busy?"

"Never too busy for you. You sure sound chipper."

Delight overtook Olivia as the truthfulness of that fact established itself into her soul. Having been miserable for so long, being chipper felt foreign to her. But she liked it. "I do, don't I?" She picked up her beverage, took a quick drink, then set it on the coffee table.

"So, how do you like it there? How's your boss? Are you enjoying your job? Did you get settled into your new place? How's Samson like it?"

"Whoa. Slow down, girl." Olivia giggled. Even though Erik, his aunt Adell, and Mickie and Virgil, and a few of the neighbors had visited frequently and had spent numerous lunches and dinners with her since she moved into her new place, she still missed her best friend something fierce. “Let me just say that I have to keep pinching myself to see if I’m dreaming or if this is really happening to me. It seems like my luck has changed.”

“Luck has nothing to do with it. God does.”

“Don’t start with that, Audra.” Olivia plunked her head on the back of the sofa and scrunched her face. The last thing she wanted to hear about was God.

Audra sighed heavily. “Okay, okay. So, back to my questions. How do you like it there?”

“I love it. You should see this place. It’s fabulous. There’s even an indoor swimming pool that Erik said I could use whenever I want to. I’ve swam in it several times already. Erik’s even joined me a couple of times.”

“Oh, really?” She could just picture Audra impersonating Groucho Marks’ waggling eyebrows. The only things missing from the image were a cigar, a black coat, a bushy mustache, and a derby hat.

“It’s not like that, Audra.” She rolled her eyes. “Oh. Oh. Guess what?”

“What?”

“Oh-h-h no.” Olivia shook her forefinger, and a smile teased her lips. “You have to guess first.”

“C’mon, Liv, just tell me. I’m too excited to guess.”

“Why are you excited? You don’t even know what it is I’m fixin’ to tell you.”

“I’m excited because,” she drew in a long breath, “I hear joy in your voice. It’s been too long.”

Yeah, it had been. Joy was something Olivia wasn’t sure she would ever feel again, and lately, she’d been feeling it quite a bit. And she had Erik to thank for it.

"C'mon tell me, please," Audra drawled out.

"Okay, you win. Okay, so," Olivia shifted further back into the chair. "The first day at work, Erik's aunt showed up, which blew me away. Mrs. Preston is the nicest lady I've ever met. She made me feel so welcome. And here's the really cool 'guess what' part." Olivia folded her legs Indian style like she had so long ago when she and Audra had shared secrets on her bed.

"His aunt came by the shop to welcome me to Charity. She even brought me a lovely basket filled with let's see," she placed her finger on her lips and squinted her eyes. "Homemade apple spice cookies, golden delicious apples, chocolate covered cashews," she paused, "crackers and cheese, apple butter, two loaves of homemade bread, a citrus candle, and three beautiful crocheted wash cloths with matching pot holders. You should see them. They're incredible.

"And then," Olivia couldn't keep the excitement from her voice, nor did she want to. "She invited me to a party. I'm not for sure, but I think the party's in my honor. Can you believe it?" Olivia ran her hand up her arm, remembering the warm hugs she'd gotten from Mrs. Preston. Nothing but her own mother's arms had ever felt so good. How she missed her mom. Olivia stopped herself. She refused to travel down that road. This was her chance for a new life, and she wasn't going to miss it.

"Wow. When is it?"

"When is what?"

"The party."

"Oh, yeah. Next Sunday at five."

"Wow. That's so awesome, Liv. And to think I was worried about you being lonely and pining away for Hammon—."

Hammond. His name drove through her heart like a sharp knife.

"Shut my mouth. Oh, Liv. I'm sorry."

Olivia grabbed one of her wayward curls and twisted it around her finger.

"I shouldn't have said that, Olivia. Forgive me." The sadness in Audra's tone disintegrated her thoughts.

"It's okay, Audie. I think moving away from Wheeling has really helped. I'm so busy with work and stuff that I've barely even thought about Hammond." *Until now that is.* Immediately she reminded herself that she was here to forget him and to get on with her life—and get on with her life she would. "Let's not talk about Hammond. Now, what else did you ask me?" She dropped the strand of hair she was twisting and switched the phone to her opposite ear.

"I asked how your boss was. Is he nice?"

Erik's image filled her mind, bringing with it a slow smile. "I can't believe how nice Erik is. He's nothing like Markus, In fact, he's gone out of his way to make me feel welcome, including eating lunch and dinner with me several times. He's wonderful."

"Wonderful, huh?"

"I told you. It's not like that, Audra." Olivia didn't stop the frustration from coming through her voice. "He's my boss and nothing else." Except a friend, perhaps. But she wouldn't tell Audra that because then Audra would have them getting married. And it would be a cold day in the Sahara desert before she'd allow that to happen. No one, not even her amazing boss would be allowed inside her closed-off heart. In fact, thinking back now, the only reason she had spent time with him was because his comment about them being friends had put her at ease.

"Anyway, we sat on the picnic table under a large oak tree and fed birds." She chuckled at the memory. "I even named one of the male cardinals Snatcher."

"Snatcher?"

"Yeah," Olivia giggled. "Every time I tossed this certain bird a small chunk of bread, it wouldn't take it. Instead, it waited until one of the other birds swooped down on it, then he'd hop over and snatch it right out of their beaks."

Audra laughed. "I have a hard time picturing you feeding birds. I remember a certain person who said they would never feed another bird as long as they lived. Even if it was starving."

"I know, I know. Hey, a gal can change her mind, can't she? Besides, feeding these birds wasn't the same as feeding that vicious parrot Aunt—" Olivia scrunched her face. "I don't want to talk about her, or her squawky, demon-possessed brat." Anger rose up inside Olivia at the mere mention of her hateful aunt. Aunt Hattie's name should have been Aunt Hate-ee for she was mean through and through. And she was the last person on earth Olivia wanted to remember.

Her aunt's selfishness had caused Olivia nearly as much grief as her parents' death. If it weren't for that wench, Olivia would have never been poor and destitute in the first place. Well, that and her ex-boss sabotaging all her job possibilities because of his malicious lies about the quality of her work. His lust-filled eyes jumped into her mind. Olivia cringed at the memory. Giving herself a mental shake, she forced her mind back to the conversation with Audra.

"I'm blown away with how kind everyone here is. Several neighbors have stopped by for a visit and to welcome me to the neighborhood. Oh, Aud, they're all so kind and generous. I can't believe how full my freezer is. There isn't room for even one more thing. My fridge is loaded with stuff too. Erik's aunt Adell keeps bringing me homemade bread. Homemade cookies, and homemade chocolate fudge with maraschino cherries and nuts.

"Good thing I have a high metabolism." Olivia giggled. "Oh, Aud," Olivia knew she was being a chatterbox, but she couldn't contain her excitement. It had been too long since she'd had anything to be excited about, so she just had to share it all with her best friend. "Adell is such a sweetheart. I've had the privilege of going to lunch with her a couple of times. She's is the most sensitive lady I've ever met. Well, besides you, that is."

Olivia grabbed a throw pillow and played with the fringe.

"We talk about quilting, gardening, baking, and traveling. You can't believe all the places that woman's been. Anyway," Olivia prattled on. "She's so careful not to bring up my past. Especially since I was so quick to change the subject the first time she asked me about it."

"You can't avoid the subject forever, Liv."

"I know that, Audra. I'm just not ready to talk about them. I came here to forget the past, remember? Well, except for you that is. So, when are you coming for a visit?"

"Actually, I was going to call you this evening because I was thinking about coming to see you next Friday. Think you could put up with me so soon?"

"Are you serious?" Olivia squealed. She swung her legs off the couch and straightened. Samson jumped, arched his back, and hissed at her.

In an attempt to calm her frightened pet, she covered the mouthpiece with her hand and crooned, "It's okay, Sammy." Samson lowered his arched back. Olivia reached down and ran her hand over his fur. The raised hair slowly went back into place, and his motor purred to life. Several calming rubs later, Samson circled a few times and then curled up in a ball.

"Yes. I'm taking two weeks off to come see my friend. I've missed you, Liv."

"Oh, Audie, I've missed you too." She focused her full attention back on her best friend. "Can't you tell? I've haven't stopped talking long enough to ask you how you are and what you've been doing since I've been gone."

"Oh, you know. Same ol' thing. Work, sleep, and eat. It's sure boring around here since you left. I can't wait to come see you. In fact, is it okay if I come and stay with you for a couple of weeks?"

"Okay?" Excitement burst through her voice. "It's more than okay."

The doorbell rang. Olivia glanced at the clock. 7:45

PM.

"Hang on a sec, Aud. Someone's at the door." Olivia laid the phone down and trotted toward the foyer.

Erik pressed the doorbell and backed up. Sitting in that big house all by himself on a Friday night was about to drive him bonkers. So, he'd decided to go for a swim. But the idea of swimming alone didn't appeal to him anymore. That's when Olivia's image in her modest one-piece bathing suit passed through his mind. Most women flaunted their goods, but not Olivia, and he respected her for that.

The doorknob turned, and the door swung open.

He couldn't keep the excitement from showing on his face. "Hi, Olivia."

Her eyes widened. "Hi."

She looked so down-to-earth standing in the doorway in knee-length gray shorts and a pink tank top. "I hope ya don't mind me stopping by, but I was bored and wondered if you'd like to go for a swim."

"Sure." Amazingly, she didn't hesitate. "Let me tell my friend I'll call 'em back later."

He glanced past her into the house. "Oh, I'm sorry. I didn't know you were busy."

She just laughed. And a pleasant sound it was. "Of course you didn't. How would you?"

Erik shifted his weight. "I should have called first. Listen, why don't you finish your call and meet me down at the pool?"

"No, no. Don't be silly. C'mon on in. I'll be just a second." Before he could respond, Olivia whirled and headed back inside, leaving her door wide open.

Erik stepped inside the air-conditioned cottage. Sweet citrus filled the air. He stood inside the foyer and watched as Olivia retrieved the phone. She covered the mouthpiece with her hand. "C'mon in and sit down. I'll be just a minute." She motioned him inside. "Hey, Aud. My boss is here. I'll call ya later okay?"

Pause.

She looked over at him and turned her back to him. "Stop it." Her voice held a threatening hint to it.

Erik felt uncomfortable eavesdropping on her conversation, but he didn't know what else to do, until he spotted Samson. He walked around the coffee table, picked up the cat, and snuggled him against his chest. "Hey, how ya doing big fella?" He rubbed the back of the cat's neck and his motor started. "Is Olivia still blaming you for her loud stomach?" He cut a glance toward Olivia, who wrinkled her nose at him.

"Okay, I'll see you next week. I can't wait."

A hint of jealousy threaded its way through his brain. See who next week? Did she have a boyfriend? He hoped not. She was the first woman he'd been really attracted to in a long time.

She hung up the phone and turned her attention on him. "I'll just get my things. Be right back." She whirled and sprinted into one of the back bedrooms.

He let out a whoosh of air and set Samson back on the couch.

Within minutes she was back, holding a towel in one hand and a large wicker looking type bag that had a huge purple flower on it in the other. “I’m ready.”

Speechless, Erik followed her to the door, forcing his eyes everywhere but on her nice looking legs.

Stepping outside, away from the air-conditioned house, heat sucked what little breath he had left from him. He never got used to the sudden temperature change. Air conditioning one minute and heat the next. You would think by eight in the evening it would cool down, but it didn’t. That pool was sounding better and better. He glanced at Olivia who had fallen into step with him.

Playfulness overtook him. “Race ya.”

She turned surprised eyes up at him, glanced toward the pool, and then took off.

“Hey, no fair,” he hollered and darted off after her. He pushed his long legs as hard as they would go but still couldn’t catch up with her. He reached the indoor pool, seconds after her, and breathlessly said, “Man, can you run.”

A smile bowed her beautiful pink lips.

Erik drew in several breaths before continuing, “Were you on the track team in school?”

Her smile clouded over leaving only that all-too-familiar sadness. Erik wondered what he had said to make her smile disappear this time. Numerous indescribable emotions skittered across her face. “Olivia, I—I.”

“Beat ya into the pool.” She swung the door open, tossed her bag and towel onto a poolside chair, and took three long steps before diving into the water.

In disbelief at how quickly she rocked from one emotion to another, Erik tossed the towel he'd been holding on a different chair and dove in. The tepid water instantly cooled his body. He opened his eyes under water and searched for Olivia. When he spotted the back of her legs, he quickly caught up to her. The urge to reach out and grab her feet tried to overpower him, but Erik knew that was too intimate, so he shoved off the bottom and made his way to the top. When he surfaced, eyes the color of the pool snagged onto his. Drops of water beaded off of Olivia's eyelashes. His finger itched to wipe them away, but again, he controlled his longing. "You, my friend, are a cheater," he accused.

She waved her arms, keeping herself suspended. "I didn't cheat. You didn't say on the count of three or anything, you just said 'race ya'. So, I did."

A spray of water flooded over his face. With one quick swipe, he removed the water from his eyes. This time he didn't control his urges. Quick as a flash, he put his hands on her head and pushed her under.

"That'll teach ya," he tossed out even though he knew she probably didn't hear him.

Erik laughed and lunged forward to swim away. As soon as his arm shot out and his hand cupped the water, Olivia grabbed his ankles, and with one yank, she pulled him under.

Olivia sprang to the surface and swam like a fish in a hurry toward the side of the pool.

Erik followed in hot pursuit. Just as she placed one foot on the poolside, Erik grabbed her ankle and pulled her backward into the water. The huge splash covered his face. He quickly brushed away the water.

Bobbing to the top of the water, she pulled her hand over her nose and mouth. “Uncle! Uncle! I give,” she rasped through a giggle.

Erik liked the sound. In fact, he liked much more than the sound. He liked her. When he first met her, she seemed so depressed and sad. But now, like this, just having fun together she was relaxed and happy. The truth was Erik could get used to having her around. While he wasn’t in love with her, he was very attracted to her—and not just physically. There was something about Olivia that drew him. Maybe it was because she seemed lost and alone. Or maybe it was the playful side of her when she knew no one was paying attention. Whatever it was, as he treaded water and watched her swimming, he knew he wanted to pursue it and find out. He also sensed that he needed to go slow and just be her friend first. Plus, he wasn’t sure how his being her boss would affect a relationship with her. He needed to be careful to not cross over that line. As she swam froggie-style toward him, one look at her beautiful turquoise eyes and he realized that wasn’t going to be easy.

Erik’s imagination took over. He pictured Olivia swimming up to him and putting her soft hands on his shoulders. He pulled her into his arms, their eyes locked and held there until his attention drifted to her mouth. Water beads covered her lips. Lips he longed to feel against his own. In slow motion, he leaned his head toward her until their parted mouths met in a warm, wet kiss. Her soft lips played with his, consuming him until…

“What’re you doing?” Olivia’s unknowing, innocent question yanked Erik back to reality.

Good grief, man. What’s wrong with you lately? And what is it about her that has you fantasizing about kissing her? He chanced a quick glance into Olivia’s eyes just an arm length away in front of him, wondering how he was going to answer her question.

Did she know what he’d been thinking? Did she sense things like his aunt Adell and Terri did? *What do they call that? Oh yeah, women’s intuition.*

“You wanna race?” Her delicate, perfect-shaped eyebrows danced teasingly at the challenge she presented him.

Now that question he could answer. “I am.” He whirled, lunged forward in a butterfly swim position, and took off.

“No fair,” she called after him.

“Hey, turnabout’s fair play,” he hollered back at her and kept going.

After swimming a few laps, they got out of the pool, toweled off, and parked their bodies on the lounge chairs. It felt so natural sitting here with her like this.

The water streaming down the cascading rock formation at the end of the pool filled the comfortable silence.

“Erik?”

"Yeah?" He turned to look at Olivia.

"Audie is coming for a visit and will be here late Friday night. I'd really love to go to your aunt's party, but it would be rude of me to leave my guest all alone."

Erik swung his legs to the side, placed his feet on the floor, and faced her. "Hey, the party's in your honor. Can't have a party if the guest of honor's not there." He smiled.

So. The party really was for her. Touched beyond measure, she fought back her burning tears.

"Bring your friend along."

"You sure Adell won't mind?" Her question came with a certain amount of uncertainty and shyness.

"Of course not. The more the merrier Aunt Adell always says."

"Would you mind calling her and making sure it's okay first, please?"

"Sure. But, I'm positive it'll be just fine." He smiled and drew in a deep breath. "Olivia?"

"Yes."

His gaze dropped, and his hesitation made her squirm. "Do you mind me asking you a personal question?" His eyes snagged on hers. Olivia wanted to know just how personal before giving her consent, but she didn't have a clue how to tell him that without sounding rude. She sucked in her lower lip and reluctantly nodded.

She scarcely drew breath while she waited for his question. A question she only hoped and prayed wouldn't have anything to do with her growing up years.

Chapter Eight

Erik's gaze captured Olivia's. "Who's Audie?"

Audie? Olivia forced her face not to show her surprise. That's what he wanted to ask her? Her lungs sucked in the air she'd deprived them of while waiting for his question.

Inside the indoor swimming pool, Olivia placed her feet on the floor. "Audie's my best friend. We grew up together. Her real name is Audra."

"I see." The relief in his eyes was evident. Olivia wondered what that was all about. "Did you grow up in Wheeling?"

"Yes. Yes I did." *Please no more personal questions,* she silently begged not wanting to take any more trips down memory lane. To make sure that didn't happen, Olivia decided to turn the tables by asking him a question. "Did you grow up in Charity?"

The light in Erik's eyes dimmed. "No." He stood and walked over to a small refrigerator.

For some odd reason, Erik chose not to elaborate. She wondered why but didn't ask. She respected that because she, too, had reasons for not wanting to answer questions about her life.

Erik bent his knees and peered into the icebox. With his back toward her, he turned his head sideways. "Would you like a Coke or some lemonade?"

"Yes, a Coke would be fine." Water dripped from her hair onto her legs. Using her fingertips, she swished a few beads of water off of her legs and sent them flying.

He reached inside the fridge and grabbed two drinks. On his way back to where she was sitting, he asked, "How many siblings do you have?"

Olivia worked her lip over. Up until now their conversations had mostly consisted of monster trucks, classic cars, the weather, his kind neighbors, feeding the birds, and their cats' silly antics. Erik of course included God in all their conversations, but not in a way that he was preaching or anything. It was just a part of who he was. He never once tried pushing religion on her, which she found both interesting and relieving.

She hated it when people asked her questions about her life, and yet she knew she couldn't avoid them forever. She also knew that she could choose how and what to answer. "I'm an only child. How 'bout you?"

He handed her a Coke and sat down. He opened a bottle for himself and took a long drink before twisting the lid back on. "I have three siblings. Slick, Tony, and Camara."

She opened her drink and took a swallow. While screwing the cap on, she wondered just how deeply she should probe into his family life. After all, if she asked him questions, then he might ask her more questions too. And she wasn't ready to talk about her past yet. Even though, for the first time in years, the burden of her past wasn't weighing as heavily on her.

Moving here had been a great idea. Audra would be amazed to find out that she actually trusted someone. Olivia herself was surprised that she felt somewhat safe after only two weeks. But she was no dummy. She would still play things by ear and still keep her guard up.

A hand waved in front of her face. She blinked.

"Earth to Olivia, come in Olivia."

The smile in his voice covered any embarrassment she might have felt at daydreaming. "Sorry, I was just thinking."

"Penny for your thoughts."

Again with the penny thing. Well, no amount of money would persuade her to tell Erik what she'd been thinking. "I can't take your penny. My penny jar is getting too heavy." A gleam accompanied her smile. "But, I want to know if Slick is your brother's real name."

"No. His real name is Daniel."

"Why do you call him Slick?"

"Because he goes through more racing slick tires than anyone we've ever known."

"Does he race monster trucks too?"

Erik chuckled. "No. Monster trucks don't have racing slicks. He runs funny cars."

"What are funny cars?" She grabbed her towel, laid it over her legs, and stared straight at Erik, realizing how much she liked the view.

"They're cars people drag race with."

"What do they look like?"

"Well," he rubbed his chin, something he did a lot. "They resemble streetcars. But they have a one-piece carbon fiber body with a tubular chassis, and the whole body raises like a hood. Whereas a regular streetcar has a straight frame and multiple working parts. Ya know, like doors, hoods, trunks. A streetcar runs between eight to three hundred horsepower. Funny cars run high performance engines with blowers, putting out thousands of horsepower. In fact, they're so quick that they have twin parachutes mounted on the back to stabilize and decelerate the car once it crosses the finish line. Otherwise, they'd burn their brakes up trying to stop."

Information overload. Olivia's mind scrambled to put a mental picture together of what they looked like based on the information Erik fed her. But, she had no idea what a tubular chassis or an engine blower was. Guess she'd have to use the computer in the shop and look it up sometime to see what they looked like.

Erik chuckled. "Funny cars are a hoot. You should go with me sometime and watch them."

"Where do they race these cars?" She kept her gaze on him while toweling off her already dry legs.

"At drag strips." His focus slid past her.

Olivia turned to see what he was looking at. Seeing nothing, she faced him and watched as a gamut of emotions shadowed his handsome face. She wanted to ask what had made him so sad, but again she didn't want to pry.

"At Swamper Speedway" he glanced at her, then turned his brown eyes away from her, staring seemingly at nothing. Seconds ticked by before he finally spoke again. "They hold drag races there all the time. Along with mud bog races, monster truck rallies, dirt bike races, and funny car events."

"Where's Swamper Speedway?"

He broke contact with whatever he was looking at and riveted his attention on her. Olivia sat up straight.

"Back home; just outside of Swamper City, Alabama."

"Oh. So you aren't from around here then?"

He unscrewed the lid to his Coke, took a long drink, and replaced the lid.

Was he going to evade her question again? It was strange how he had a way of answering but not really answering. Just like someone else she knew—herself.

"No." That bit of information shocked her. "I moved here not too long ago." The pensive look on his face never left.

As much as she was afraid of giving him an opening into her life, she really wanted to know about his. "What brought you to West Virginia?"

"Well," he pressed his hand over his mouth and down his chin. "I was tired of the everyday ho-hum of running one of Dad's dealerships and wanted some adventure."

Lands o' Goshen, Olivia inwardly cringed. *Another adventure, seeking male. What's up with men and their desire for adventure? Oh, and like you never craved it*, Olivia chastised herself. She had, but after Hammond disappeared, her audacious spirit no longer existed. Well, perhaps it did a little, but only a little. But she had no intentions of allowing it back into her life. She focused her attention back on Erik.

"The restlessness inside of me was really starting to get me down. So, when I came out here to West Virginia for a monster truck rally at the Charleston Civic Center, this indescribable peace came over me. I asked the Lord why," Erik quirked his lip sideways and released a quick snort. "But I already knew why. For some reason, the Lord wanted me to leave my home and move here." His gaze locked on hers. "Who knows? Maybe it was so we could connect."

Connect? Olivia blinked, not liking the sound of that at all. *Connect in what way?* She swallowed hard, trying to force down the fear that accompanied Erik's words.

♥ ♥ ♥

Erik caught the glimpse of fear in Olivia's eyes and instantly knew what he'd said to put it there. Hoping to reassure her, he laid his hand on top of hers.

She glanced down at their hands and then back at him. Wrinkles marred her forehead.

Realizing that was the wrong thing to do to the woman sitting directly across from him, who now resembled a frightened little bird, he raised his hand, backed off, and rubbed the back of his neck. Remembering he should keep his distance was becoming increasingly difficult. "Ya know. If I would have never moved here, then you wouldn't have come for the job interview. And I would have never found someone who knew exactly the kind of design I was looking for on my monster truck. That's all I meant." *Well, that's all I'm going to tell you anyway.* He couldn't stop his mouth from smiling.

Her stiff body relaxed, and the wrinkles around her

eyes disappeared.

Good. His words and smile had accomplished their job.

The fear on her face turned into a soft quizzical look. "Do you like it here?"

Her question threw him off guard. Did he like it here? He missed his family something fierce. He loved spending time with his aunt Adell, and the people in West Virginia were super friendly. But, he was lonely. He looked at the beautiful woman sitting in front of him and realized since she had arrived he wasn't nearly as lonely as he had been. "I do now."

Her eyes widened. Panic gripped him. He'd better clarify what he meant, or the little frightened bird in Olivia would spread its wings and take flight. "I'm so glad you're here, Olivia. I really needed a friend."

Olivia couldn't keep the relief of his words from showing up on her face. Knowing Erik saw them as nothing more than friends put her at ease. "Thanks. I'm glad I'm here too." And she meant it. She picked up the towel and dabbed the water drops trickling down her arms from her wet hair.

Seeing how Erik no longer looked sad, she decided to change the subject. "So, are you and Slick the only ones in your family who race?"

"No, Camara does too."

"What does she race?"

"Mud boggers."

"Mud boggers?" She tilted her head. "What are those?" As he explained, Olivia listened intently. She didn't understand most of what he said, but he was right, it was nice to have a friend. "I'd love to see one. Where does she race?"

"Mostly at Swamper Speedway. But sometimes, she and her husband Chase run at other places. In fact, they're coming next weekend." His pearly whites sparkled. "I've invited several local boys and people from back home to come to the mud bog race. My monster truck buddies will be coming too. I can hardly wait." Something about Erik's animated face reminded her of Hammond's, right before he'd left for the hot air balloon races.

Her hand pressed against her stomach as if to squash the pit that now filled it. The last thing she wanted to do was dwell on that wretched day Hammond had left or, the big fight they'd gotten into. She and her mother had gotten into a huge fight the day her parents had left too. Neither of them had returned home. Again with the dreaded déjà vu. Just when things were going so well, why did her past have to raise its ugly head?

Oblivious to her tormenting thoughts and much to her relief, Erik continued, "This will be the first year I'll be holding them on my place."

"Here?" Olivia looked outside the floor to ceiling glass windows. "Where?"

"Oh, that's right. I've never shown you my race track, have I?"

"No." *He has his own racetrack? Is there anything he doesn't have?*

"Well, we'll just have to change that then, won't we? How about tomorrow morning I show you around the place?"

"Sounds great." And it really did.

"Good. I'll pick you up at eight a.m. sharp." He finished his drink.

"Well, it's getting late. I'd better go." She stood and picked up her things, then turned to say goodnight. Erik was so close, she took a stumbling step backward. She had to force herself to not stare at his bronzed, muscular physique.

"Let me walk you back. It's dark out." Those gorgeous brown eyes of his bore into her.

Did he have to look so good? Even worse, did she have to keep noticing how good looking he was and how well built he was? The need to distance herself from him pressed in on her. "No, that's okay. I'll be fine. But thanks anyway."

He collected his towel. "Well, you'll have to forgive me, Olivia. But my mama raised me to be a gentleman, and if she ever found out that I let you walk back to your house, in the dark, unattended, she'd have my backside in a wringer."

So much for distancing herself from him. Olivia planted a hand on her waist. "Boy, the women in your life must be hazardous to your health." She smirked. "Mickie would skin your hide and your mother's gonna put your backside in a wringer. Lands o' Goshen, I can only imagine what your girlfriend is like." With those words she sprinted toward her cottage, leaving Erik behind.

Chapter Nine

The following Friday, Erik insisted Olivia take the day off. All week long, she'd worked like a mad woman, twelve-hour days, fifteen-minute lunches trying to get at least one of his monster truck bodies completely finished, which she had. She so wanted to work longer to get one more completed, but Erik wouldn't hear of it.

In a way she was relieved because she desperately needed to go shopping for new clothes. And this morning she'd done just that. And now, here she was at Erik's racetrack, standing in front of a huge Dodge truck with the words *X-Rivals Domination* in bold white letters on the door. The same type of lettering, with the words *See Ya* were on another truck parked next to the Dodge. Never having actually gone to any auto races before, let alone being in the contestants' pit, she marveled at everything around her.

Every type of vehicle, from a Willy's jeep, to a Chevy Blazer, to a Ford Ranger, filled the contestants' pit. All of them sat high off the ground with huge tires. Each had a different name on either the door, the rear bumper, the back windshield, or on their hood somewhere. Several revved their engines. The loud crackling sound tickled her insides and vibrated her eardrums. But she didn't mind. Too bad Audra wasn't here to see all this. She would love it. But, her plane wouldn't come in until around ten o'clock that evening.

"Hello. You must be Olivia." A small petite blonde with a strong southern drawl extended her hand toward Olivia.

Olivia met her handshake, wondering who the little beauty with the yellow Chevy cap was.

"Olivia," Erik said from beside her. She glanced at him when the warmth of his hand found the small of her back. "This is my sister, Camara." Olivia looked back at her. "Camara, this is my friend Olivia."

Camara smiled and embraced her like she was someone special. "It's so nice to meet you, Olivia."

"Hey, Erik." Erik swung toward the sound of the handsome man with spiked hair and a physique to die for. Just like Erik's.

He grabbed him in a bear hug. When he let Erik go, the man stepped over to Camara, put his arm around her, and kissed her smack dab on the lips, and let his mouth linger for a few moments. Then his attention threaded its way to Olivia. "You must be Olivia."

"And you must be Chase," she responded.

"How'd ya know?"

She smiled. "Well, if you aren't Chase, then Camara has a lot of explaining to do."

For a moment, Chase looked befuddled. Then he glanced at his wife's lips. "Ah. I get it." As if to prove he really did get it, he kissed his wife again.

A voice came over the intercom. "Drivers get ready."

Camara scurried over to Olivia. "Listen, we have to go

now. But if you aren't doing anything after the races, would you and Erik like to go have dinner with Chase and me?"

Olivia didn't know what to say. So she looked at Erik, waiting for his reply.

"Sounds great, sis."

"Okay, we'll see ya later then." She spun, took two steps and turned back. "I'm so happy you're here. Erik talks about you all the time."

Olivia looked at Erik with questioning eyes.

He shrugged sheepishly. "My little sister has a big mouth. I'm sorry if she's given you the wrong impression. You'll have to forgive me, but I can't stop bragging about what nice work you do. I interviewed a lot of people for your job, but none of their work came even close to the expert quality of yours. Plus, I've had a blast these past three weeks. When you live so far out of town, it gets pretty lonely in the evenings. And," he smiled at her, "I've really enjoyed our swims. I hate swimming alone. It really is nice having a friend to do things with." Erik wrapped his hand around hers. "C'mon, let's grab some chairs and watch the races."

Olivia marveled that she didn't mind the feel of his hand over hers. Of course, knowing he thought of her as only a friend helped. Hand-in-hand, she allowed him to lead her toward his pickup where he unlocked the diamond cut toolbox and retrieved two long canvas tubes with folding chairs. The guy really did love blue.

After grabbing two Cokes from the cooler, they made their way to the orange barricade fence and set up their chairs.

"You don't have to help with anything?" Olivia asked.

"Nope. That's what I pay people for. I wanted to enjoy spending time with Camara and Chase." He paused. "And you." This time his smile touched a place deep inside her.

Not liking the sensation, Olivia focused her attention on the announcer's voice as he said that Chase and Camara Lamar were to line up at the pits. "They have to race against each other?" she asked Erik even though she wanted to look anywhere but at him right now. That sensation hadn't left her yet, and she didn't like or want it hanging around. Unfortunately, she really wanted to know the answer to her question and it would be rude not to look at him.

"Yes and no. This is a timed event."

"But don't they," she tilted her head and shrugged. "ya know. Like fight over who wins? I mean, how could you compete against your own spouse?" Olivia didn't get it. That would be completely weird. "Doesn't that make for a strained atmosphere at home?"

Erik laughed. "Well, it would have if it hadn't been for God."

"God?" She scrunched her nose in disgust. "What on earth does God have to do with them mud bog racing?"

He chuckled, and when he did, the edges of his eyes crinkled. "Well, it's a long story. I'll just give you the nutshell version. Camara and Chase were big time rivals. They both fought to prove how great they were to the other one until an accident nearly killed Camara."

Horrified, Olivia's hand flew to her mouth.

"The fact that she's even alive today is a miracle. But the biggest miracle out of that whole mess was Chase's dad accepted the Lord, and his family reunited. Plus, they learned that winning wasn't everything. Now don't get me wrong, they still like to win. But before her accident, I think what they enjoyed more than racing was trying to out do the other. The sad part is, their foolish pride nearly cost Camara her life. But, praise God. He didn't let that happen. A lot of people were praying for her. And now the two of them are happy campers. They're doing what they love, building bog trucks, and racing them. They're just doing it together now."

Olivia wondered if Erik would still talk about God so generously if things would have turned out differently for Camara and his prayers went unanswered like hers had. As much as she hated what was happening inside her, she was powerless to stop the bitter well of anger spewing its venomous poison through her wounded heart. For as long as Olivia drew breath, she would never understand why God took some people's loved ones and not others.

Oh, she'd heard all the reasons *why* by well meaning Christians. But none of their reasons ever made sense. As far as Olivia was concerned, prayer was like a roulette wheel. Toss your request onto the prayer wheel, and maybe, just maybe, if you're lucky enough, that prayer might land in the answer prayer slot. Well, luck was sorely lacking in her life because everyone she loved had been ripped from her even though she'd earnestly prayed and believed God to spare them.

Like a cancer, the thought of someone else's prayers

getting answered and not hers, ate away at her soul. Why had God spared Camara and not her parents? Or her grandma? Or Hammond? While she was happy for Erik that Camara hadn't died, she couldn't stop the battle raging inside her why some lived and others didn't.

And would those same people still think as highly of God as they did if He hadn't answered their prayers? After all, it would be easy to love God when you had a loving family, a warm bed, food, enough money that you never had to worry again where your next meal was coming from. Erik had all of that. People loved him. The man had probably never seen a day's tragedy like she had. When her parents were alive and things were going well, it had been easy for her to serve God and to love Him. But when life struck her several deadly blows—

Olivia wondered. Would Erik still serve God if something bad happened to someone he loved? Remorse the size of a Mack truck crashed into Olivia for even allowing herself to think such vile things. Sick and tired of dwelling on the negative, she forced her attention back to Erik.

"What the devil means for evil, God turns it around for good."

What? She blinked. *What was he talking about?* She should have been paying attention again instead of allowing her mind to visit the indelible dark caves of the past.

Her mind scrambled to recall what Erik had said. It was something like… Oh yeah. "What the devil means for evil, God turns it around for good." If that were true, then why hadn't God done that in her life?

Then, like the wind riding on the breeze, the thought that God *had* turned what Satan meant for her evil into something good, blew across her soul. She now had a great job, a beautiful home, and as she looked at Erik, a wonderful friend. For the first time in ages, Olivia wondered if God had indeed taken what was meant for her destruction and turned it into good. But how could that be? No, somehow He was punishing her as He always did. It was just that she couldn't quite see how this time.

Her concentration switched gears when the truck next to them revved its engine. She'd ponder on that later.

Erik leaned into Olivia and talked close to her ear. "See the Dodge truck Chase is driving?"

Olivia turned her attention toward the truck lining up at the long mud-filled pit. "Yeah."

"Before they got married, they built that truck together. On their wedding day, they ran it through the mud pit."

"You're kidding?" She spun her head and nearly collided noses with Erik. Her gaze shot to his before she jerked her face back. "Sorry."

"Hey, no problem."

Not understanding the twinkle in his eyes, Olivia decided it was best to leave it alone.

"Nope. Before all the guests left, everyone went outside. I timed them while they flew through the pit."

"That's too funny. Is that all they do then? Build and drive bog trucks?"

"Well, that and other things. Chase and Camara

opened up their own mechanic shop. Together they build boggers, restore classic cars, and do auto repairs. They love it."

Quick as lightning Erik pushed himself up from the chair. "Here they go."

Olivia jumped up and stood next to him. The roar of the engines sent a tingle up and down her spine. Mud slung in the air twenty feet or more. Camara and Chase were neck-and-neck.

Never taking her eyes off of the bog vehicles, Olivia stood on her tiptoes and yelled close to Erik's ear. "How can they see? Their windshields are covered in mud."

Before he could answer, the trucks were at the end of the mud pit, flying up and out, and the announcer's voice came over the intercom.

"Chase Lamar's time is 6.7. Camara's time is 6.5."

Erik grabbed her hand again and off he went. Olivia hurried to keep in step with him as they made their way back to where the contestants were parked. Camara and Chase drove slowly toward them and stopped. They revved their engines and shut them off. Olivia instantly missed the loud noise. There was something so masterful about it.

Both removed their harnesses and helmets, hopped out, and ran to each other. Mud covered their arms and splattered across their chins and clothing, but that didn't seem to bother them because they threw their arms around each other and shared a muddy kiss.

Olivia quickly looked away, certain her cheeks were as red as the truck Camara drove.

"Great job, baby." Chase praised Camara.

"You, too, sweetie." Camara returned. They hugged and kissed again.

Olivia dropped her chin, slanted her head sideways, and looked over at Erik, wondering if he was as uncomfortable with the exchange as she was. He didn't look at all fazed. Instead, a grin spread across his face. When Erik's feet moved, she glanced up.

Erik swooped up his sister and swung her around. "Way to go, sis!" He set her down, then grabbed Chase and gave him a quick hug. He too, didn't seem to mind the mud.

As they talked, loneliness and sadness vacillated across Olivia's heart. How she missed her parents. How she longed to be part of a family like this. Erik was one lucky man.

Erik darted a glance her way, then did a double take before heading over toward her. "Sorry."

"For what?" Olivia blinked.

"For ignoring you."

Olivia waved her hand once. "That's okay."

"No, it isn't." He glanced back at Camara and Chase who had fallen into their post run rituals. "You look like something's bothering you. Are you—"

Olivia jerked up her forefinger and pointed it at him. "Don't say it. And don't insult me by offering me a penny for my thoughts either."

Erik's forehead wrinkled.

"If you're going to offer me money for my thoughts…" Olivia held her finger to her lips and acted like she was really concentrating hard. "Let see. With inflation the way it is, I think you should at least offer me six-bits." She rubbed her chin. "Yeah," she nodded once. "Six-bits just might do it."

Merriment crossed through Erik's eyes and then made its way to his mouth. He nodded and chuckled. "Well, I was going to offer you a dollar. But, hey, you said seventy-five cents. The way I figure," he crossed his arms over his barreled chest. "I'm gettin' off cheap. So, how 'bout it?"

"How about what?" Olivia shrugged, feigning ignorance.

Erik dug in his front pants pocket. Change jingled as he dug around. Pulling his hand out, he flicked his way through his change and collected four quarters, two dimes, and a nickel. "Here. A dollar twenty-five should be a fair enough price for your thoughts." He grabbed her hand and laid the change in her palm, curling her fingers over the money.

"That's more than six-bits. But I'll take it." Olivia opened up her palm and pressed her finger over the quarter. "Twenty-five." She touched the second quarter. "Fifty." The next quarter. "Seventy-five." Another quarter. "One dollar." She flicked at the dimes. "One ten. One twenty." And finally the nickel. "One twenty-five. Okay. It's all there." She put the money in her jeans pocket and blankly stared up at him. "Lands o' Goshen. I forgot what I was thinking."

"Hey. No thoughts. No money." He held his hand out to receive the coinage back.

"I have news for you, sir." She sent him her sweetest smile. "I never planned on telling you what I was thinking." She whirled. "I just wanted a snow cone." She laughed, then quickly sprinted toward the concession stand.

Chapter Ten

On the way to the restaurant, every time Erik thought about Olivia and the snow cone, his insides shook with quiet laughter. The more relaxed Olivia became, the more her fun side appeared. There were times, however, when sadness still shadowed her face. Something in her past had obviously caused her a lot of grief. In time, Erik hoped she would feel comfortable enough with him to share. After all, sharing one's burdens helps lessen the load. Erik sensed her load was heavy.

He turned his pickup into the restaurant parking lot, pulled in next to Chase and Camara's rig, and threw his vehicle in park.

"You're sure lucky to have family."

Erik barely heard her for the softness in her voice. "No, Olivia." He shut the engine off and removed his keys.

She jerked her head so fast his direction he thought surely she'd snapped her neck.

"I'm blessed. Luck has nothing to do with it." At her frown he wondered if he should say something else. But the tug in his spirit let him know to be quiet.

But there was nothing quiet about Olivia's stomach when it rumbled.

"There's that Roseman woman growl again." He chuckled. "Humph. And I thought my monster truck was loud. It's definitely no match for that stomach of yours. In fact," he glanced in the direction of his sister and lowered his voice in a conspiratorial whisper, "I think Camara and Chase heard it too."

Her attention flew toward them, standing at the front of his pickup closest to the passenger side. Erik laughed because they weren't even paying any attention to them.

"That was mean." The mock glare she gave him made him laugh harder. She opened her door and slid out before he had a chance to go around and help her. Good thing his mother wasn't around. She'd give him a tongue lashing for sure. He got out, hit the lock button on his keys, and pocketed them. Tonight was certain to be interesting and fun.

On the walk toward the front of the restaurant Olivia marveled at how comfortable she felt around these people. Only three weeks had passed, and yet it was as if she'd known Erik and his family forever. Even more amazing was how the weight of the past was slipping further and further away. It still hurt thinking about her parents and Hammond, but she no longer dwelled on it until the melancholy suffocated her like before. Now when she thought of things, Erik seemed to sense her sadness and did something to lift her droopy spirit.

Camara looped elbows with Olivia. The intimate gesture blessed her. *Blessed?* That word hadn't entered her vocabulary for years. Erik was definitely rubbing off on her.

"I can't wait to eat. I'm famished. How 'bout you?" Camara asked.

At the mention of eating, Olivia's stomach thundered.

Camara looked over at her and started laughing. "Guess that answers my question."

"I heard that," Erik said from behind them.

Olivia looked over her shoulder. "Your ears are playin' tricks on ya." Her cheeks warmed.

Erik fell in step beside Olivia. Chase followed suit with Camara, then he leaned his head forward and looked directly at Olivia. "Well then, my ears must be playin' tricks on me too. If I didn't know better, I'd have thought someone fired up a bog truck." He laughed good-naturedly.

While embarrassed over her Roseman stomach, Olivia loved the easy camaraderie. "What can I say? It's a family curse."

"Oh, but a cute one," Erik said next to her ear.

Erik opened the restaurant door and waited while everyone preceded him inside. A male host led them to a table next to a window. Erik held Olivia's chair out for her, waited for her to be seated, then settled into the chair beside her.

Olivia looked out the window. Moonlight cast its golden glow along with the rainbow lights rippling through the giant three-tiered water fountain. Full-embodied lions were on the bottom, and the next two layers were lion heads. Water poured from each lion's mouth. Four lady statues holding water jugs with water streaming out them set on the brick edge of the fountain. While it was completely different from the fountain in Hammond's back yard, it reminded Olivia how at Christmastime, Hammond would change the white lights to red and green. He loved Christmas. It was his favorite time of the year. Olivia waited for the sadness to come with the memory, but it didn't.

"It is beautiful, isn't it?"

She turned toward Erik, and once again their noses nearly collided. This time, however, she didn't jerk back, but slowly moved away. "It sure is."

A waitress with long red hair and blue eyes brought their menus. Knowing Erik's love for blue, she wondered if he noticed her. One glance at him revealed his indifference. That surprised her because if Hammond were here now, he would be drooling all over her. The fact that Erik didn't lifted her heart.

Olivia grabbed her menu and leaned back in her chair. While studying the prices on the menu, joy flooded the very essence of her soul. This time she didn't have to calculate how much money she had or didn't have. Three weeks of pay filled her checkbook quite nicely. Erik had refused to let her pay any rent or utilities in spite of all her claims that it wasn't right. Instead, he just smiled and said they would work out the details later. And they would too. She'd see to it. Because of his generosity, a small wad of bills lined the bottom of her pocket. They felt glorious.

"What are ya gonna have, Olivia?"

She peered over the menu at Camara. "I'm not sure. Erik," she turned questioning eyes at him. "What do you recommend?"

Her eyes connected with his for the briefest of moments before her gaze fell to her menu.

"The fried trout and morel mushrooms is really good. So is the grilled Alaskan salmon with roasted red potatoes and southern style green beans. And if you're really adventurous you can try the wild boar ribs."

"Wild boar ribs!" Her wide eyes flew back to him. She knew that a fly could land on her tongue if she didn't shut her mouth, but the idea of eating wild boar ribs grossed her out "Ew. Ew. Ew." She shuddered.

His smile did little to calm her repulsion. "I'm just teasin' ya. They're really good."

Olivia set aside her menu. "I'll take your word for it." She wrinkled her nose and pressed her lips tight.

The waitress returned to their table with pen and pad in hand and smiled coquettishly at Erik. "May I take your order?"

"Go ahead," Erik said to Olivia.

Miss Red's smile dropped when she faced Olivia.

"I'll have the sliced ham with apples, a cup of bacon potato soup, and lemonade, please." Olivia flashed the woman her most winsome smile.

The waitress's eyes narrowed, then brightened when she turned toward Erik. Flirtatiously, she smiled at him and lowered her eyelashes in a sultry manner. "And for you, Sir?"

The woman's blatant wantonness sent shockwaves throughout Olivia's brain. Flashbacks of Hammond and how he used to openly flirt with every pretty waitress right in front of her, assaulted her mind. Confusion fogged her brain. Years ago, when her life had felt as empty as a black hole, Hammond, her knight in shining armor, had ridden up on his white steed, or in this case, his white Corvette, had scooped her up, and taken her on a trip to fantasyland. Or had he? Yes. Yes he had. Hammond was the biggest sweetheart ever. His only major flaw was he loved to flirt.

Olivia pulled her thoughts back from the past and fastened them onto the present. Onto Erik to be exact.

"I'll have the Alaskan Salmon," Erik said, instantly looking away from the woman. He seemed impervious to her, even though she was clearly not impervious to him.

After all of their orders were taken and the waitress left, Camara laid her arms on the table and leaned toward Olivia. "Erik says you're from Wheeling."

"Yes, that's right." She braced herself for the dreaded questions that were certain to follow.

"Do you ever go to any mud bog races out there?"

Well that wasn't what she expected. "No, I've never even heard of mud bog racing until I moved here. Besides, Hammond wasn't into auto racing and stuff."

"Who's Hammond?" Erik asked, completely ignoring the waitress who paused longer than necessary while placing Erik's drink in front of him. When the blue-eyed woman realized he wasn't paying any attention to her, she finished serving the others their drinks and left.

Olivia made the mistake of looking at Erik's expectant face. A silent battled warred inside her. Stalling for time, she grabbed her freshly made lemonade, brought it to her lips, and slowly sipped the sweet and sour drink. Sooner or later, she knew people would ask about her past, but she just wasn't sure how much to tell them. If she said he was her fiancé, would they want to know more? And anything other than that would be a lie. Not one to speak falsehoods, she opted for the truth. "He was my fiancé." She focused on the moisture dripping down her glass, then took another drink. The ice-cold beverage, slid down her throat as she gulped several swallows, nearly giving herself a brain freeze.

All eyes were on her. Desperate to get the spotlight off of her, she set her drink down and picked up her cloth napkin. "Camara." She wiped her hands, then spread the napkin on her lap. "What made you decide to become a mechanic and race bog trucks? Had you always enjoyed messing with vehicles, or what?"

Everyone's attention turned toward Camara. Everyone's, she noticed with some disconcertedness, but Erik's. Olivia fought not to notice that it took him a full minute to shift his focus off of her and put it on his sister.

Camara's eyes lit up as she explained how she'd gotten started. Her arms told the story right along with her voice. "It was all his fault, ya know." She jerked her thumb toward Erik, knocking her sweetened tea glass over. At once, all four of them tossed their napkins on the brown liquid spreading across the table. Olivia's thoughts flew back to that first day in Erik's office. Again with the déjà vu. Only this time, Camara was the one sopping up the mess and not her.

After the drink was corralled, Olivia faced her boss. "Okay, Erik. It's your turn."

One of his eyebrows spiked. "My turn to what?"

"To spill your drink."

"Huh?"

"Remember the day of my interview whenever I spilled coffee all over your desk. Your secretary said you are forever spilling your drink. Well, now's a perfect time." Mirth danced in her eyes and lips. "By the way, did she ever buy you that spill-proof cup?" She pressed her lips together to keep from laughing.

Erik dunked his fingertips in his water and flicked it at her.

"Hey, no fair." Olivia dipped her fingers in her lemonade and flicked it at him.

"Okay, you two. Behave," Chase warned.

Guilt colored her cheeks as she shot a glance at Erik, Chase, and Camara.

"Yeah, behave." A smirk twisted Camara's lips. "Don't y'all know that it's poor table manners to do," she dipped her fingers in Chase's tea, "this?" She flicked her fingers toward her husband.

"Oh, yeah?" Chase imitated his wife by flicking his drink at her.

A giggle formed in Olivia's stomach. Gaining momentum, it turned into a full-blown belly laugh. The waitress stepped up to the table with their food and looked at them as if they were insane. Everyone straightened in their chairs and feigned innocence. Everyone but Olivia. She covered her mouth with her napkin, tilted her head down, and strained her eyes upward. Although no sound came out of her mouth, her shaking shoulders were a dead give-away that she was still laughing.

As the waitress set their plates in front of them, she noticed the spill and gave Olivia a dirty look before she started gathering up the soiled napkins. That did it. Olivia lost it. A case of the giggles overtook her, and there was nothing she could do to stop them. Nor did she want to. It felt wonderful to laugh again. Several moments later, with everyone still watching her, she excused herself and headed toward the ladies room. Standing in front of the mirror, palms resting on the burgundy marble countertop, she leaned forward to examine her eye makeup. But her makeup wasn't what she noticed. Staring back at her was something she hadn't seen in years. A radiant, happy face.

She grabbed a napkin out of the basket lying on the vanity and dabbed at the moisture in her eyes. So was this what true joy felt like?

Chapter Eleven

Olivia was grateful Erik offered to drive her to the airport outside of Beckley to pick up Audra. Getting lost in the dark was not her idea of fun. She sat quietly in Erik's pickup, marveling at her newfound happiness. Only three weeks in this man's presence had her experiencing more joy than she had in the last sixteen years of her life. Amazing what one sensitive, kind man could do.

Hammond had been like that too. Especially after her Aunt Hattie had disappeared. He never once criticized Olivia or judged her for not caring about the old bat. Cruel as it sounded, the only thing Olivia had cared about was that she didn't care at all. Hardness of heart frightened her. And yet a hard heart was exactly what she'd gotten over the years. But then again, anyone who had to live with the likes of her wicked aunt wouldn't care either. Of that fact, Olivia was certain. She had lost track of the number of times she'd ended up in the emergency room with broken bones.

Whenever the doctors had taken her into another room, away from her aunt's earshot, to question her, her aunt's threats had ticker-taped through her wounded soul. Like her aunt's trained parrot, Olivia mimicked everything her aunt had programmed her to say. It was safer that way.

Several times over the years she'd thought about running away. But then her aunt's warning that if she ever tried to run away she'd find her and make her "pay dearly" kept her from actually doing it. Without a doubt, Olivia knew her aunt would follow through with her vicious threats.

"Penny for your thoughts."

Saved from taking more of the depressing trip down the black corridors of time, she felt Erik's low tone wrap around her like the safety of her mother's arms used to.

She shifted in the truck seat as much as the seatbelt allowed and playfully turned the question on him. "You mean you'd trust me with more of your money after I gypped you out of a dollar twenty-five?"

Erik raised his finger and shook it at her. "You've got a point there, ma'am."

"Ma'am?" Her brows reached for the sky. "Lands o' Goshen, you make me sound like an old lady." Olivia chuckled at the irony of her words because Lands o' Goshen was something her Grandmother used to say.

"Where'd you say you came up with that saying?"

"It was Mimi's," she paused, "my grandma's favorite saying. It took me a long time to figure out what it meant until Mimi showed me in her Bible that Goshen was where Moses was from. I still didn't get why she used it, but it's a part of her and something I remember about her, so I use it."

"Where's your grandma now?" He glanced at her, then back at the road. "Does she live in Wheeling?"

Olivia turned back in her seat and gazed forward. "No. Mimi died when I was ten. She had a heart attack when she heard the news of my parents' death—" Olivia's gaze bolted toward Erik. She couldn't believe she'd just told him her parents were dead. The risk of someone finding out that she was responsible for their demise made her shudder inwardly with fear. She had moved to Charity to get away from her past and to forget it, not to have it ruin the best thing that had ever happened to her. But really, that was stupid. The past was there whether she wanted it to be or not.

"I'm sorry, Olivia." He reached over, slid his hand under hers, and curled his fingers over the top of hers. The warmth of his words, and his gentle squeeze gave her the comfort she desperately needed. And right now, she needed the connection more than she cared to admit. And that scared her.

As if he sensed her need for silence, he remained quiet. The only connection between the two of them was their clasped hands.

The closer they got to the airport somewhere off in the darkness, the more fidgety Olivia became. The last two times she'd been at an airport had not ended so well. One of those times, she and Hammond had gotten into a huge fight, and she never saw him alive again. The other time, she and her parents had argued, and when they boarded their friend's private plane, she had never seen them alive again either. Both times, life as she had always known it had ceased to exist for her.

At the time of her parents' death, the only comfort she had in the midst of all the tragedy was that her beloved Mimi would be caring for her. That sole comfort only lasted a few days, however, because after her parents' death, the sixty-year-old woman's heart just couldn't take the shock that her only daughter was dead.

Memories of crying for days with no rest in sight invaded her mind. Every molecule in Olivia's body had hurt. Headaches and eye pain were her constant unwanted companions. But the biggest pain came from way deep inside her spirit. God, Whom she had adored, had let her down in her biggest time of need. Didn't He know that a ten-year-old girl needed her mother? Needed her father? Her grandmother? If He had, He certainly didn't care because they were all gone within a matter of days. And she alone was left behind with a gaping hole so big that even the entire universe couldn't fill it.

She'd cried rivers of tears, but they never brought her loved ones back. A well-meaning neighbor lady told Olivia that the Bible said God puts our tears in a bottle. Was that supposed to comfort a ten-year-old? All Olivia thought was God must have one gigantic bottle with her name plastered on it.

The real shocker came the day Olivia had discovered that an aunt she didn't even know existed until the woman read about her parents' death in the newspaper would be her guardian. Whatever a guardian was. The judge explained to Olivia that her aunt would move in with her because she wanted to take care of her. Boy was he wrong. It wasn't Olivia Aunt Hattie wanted to take care of. She only wanted to take care of herself…using Olivia and her money.

Thoughts of her aunt folded over Olivia, smothering the breath from her lungs as the darkness of the pit she'd lived in for so long closed around her. Only Erik's hand still in hers reassured her that the nightmare might finally be over. Still, the dark memories crowded in around her, pressing ever heavier. Like how years later, Olivia discovered how her shrewd aunt had even fooled the courts. By law, her aunt was to send in a quarterly report to the court, accounting for every penny spent. Aunt Hattie turned in the reports, but she lied about the expenses. Yearly clothing, six thousand dollars? What a joke that was. Olivia wore hand-me-downs from a dumpy old thrift store.

As if all of that wasn't bad enough, one day shortly after her sixteenth birthday, Olivia arrived home from a particularly hard day at school, only to find a large moving van parked in her driveway, and people moving furniture into her house.

Fear propelled her forward. "What are you doing?" she demanded with a boldness she didn't even know she possessed.

The elderly man's eyes widened. He smiled. "I'm moving into my new home."

"*Your* new home." Olivia gulped in several breaths as she stood there clutching her books. "This is *my* home." She dashed past the man and raced into the house. Frantically running from room to room, she discovered everything, including all of her personal belongings were gone.

That morning when she'd left for school, she had a whole houseful of furniture and things. Her things. And by the time she got home, everything was gone. All of her mother's china, her mother's jewelry, her mother's books, their family photo albums, everything—gone. Not one memento of her parents remained anywhere in the house.

The elderly gentleman walked up beside her. "Where—where'd my things go?" Her voice cracked under the strain.

The man shrugged, looking as confused as she was. "I saw one of those non-profit organization vans removing stuff earlier. I'm sorry I didn't pay attention to the name or you could call them and see if they know where your stuff went."

The floor collected Olivia into its cold arms. Tears poured from her. As if she were reliving her parents' deaths all over again, pain sliced through every part of her being… spirit… soul… and body. Not only were her parents gone, but their things were gone as well. She had no home, no clothes, and no money.

Desperate to get away from all the painful memories, she forced strength into her legs, jumped up, steadied herself, and fled from the house.

Mindlessly wandering around the neighborhood, she questioned everything—especially the sanity of believing in a loving, caring God. Her words to Him at that moment still echoed in her battered heart. "God, I begged You to forgive me for what I said to Mom. I didn't mean it. I don't know what else I can say or do so that You'll stop punishing me. Pastor Mannon said You punish those You love." With the back of her hand, she swiped the tears trekking down her cheeks. "I don't want You to love me anymore, God. I can't take anymore pain. So do me a favor, and please leave me alone."

Tired and hungry, she finally made her way to Audra's house. When they found out that she would be placed into a foster home until she turned eighteen, they convinced the courts that they would love to have her stay with them.

Even after she got a job and found a decent place to stay, she spent hours at their house until Audra bought her hair salon and moved into her own tiny apartment.

Later on, when Olivia lost her job after Hammond's disappearance, she could no longer afford her two-room flat. Audra had offered for her to come and stay at her place, but it was already crammed full with Audra's belongings.

So rather than burden her friend by adding even more stuff to the already over-crowded place, Olivia had moved into her rundown apartment, where she had stayed despite the horrible conditions. Olivia knew if Audra ever saw where and how she lived, her friend would personally pack her up and move her in to her apartment, regardless of how cramped it would be. So Olivia had always managed to meet Audra somewhere or the two of them ended up at Audra's place. No matter what, Olivia refused to let Audra see that apartment even though many nights she'd awakened to find ginormous cockroaches crawling on her or her aching stomach growling from hunger. Audra would have been appalled to know that Olivia had gone for days with very little to eat, but she didn't want her friend to bear the responsibility for her rotten life. It was her problem, not Audra's.

Besides, crummy living conditions were only part of

the horror that life had become. Nightmares about plane crashes and dead bodies invaded many a sleep. That same hellish dream replayed through her mind more nights than not.

"Mommy, Daddy, don't leave me. Please don't leave me." Fear thrashed at her mind.

A witch suddenly appeared, flying about on a broom, zipping past her. Olivia whirled, desperately trying to follow the black-cloaked woman with the pointed hat. Her tiny heart raced, feeling like it would explode. Her eyes snagged onto the woman's face. She opened her mouth to scream, but no sound came forth. Aunt Hattie's wicked smile and devilish eyes flashed in front of her. Poof! The image evaporated.

Olivia whirled trying to find her, but all she saw through the darkness were dead bodies appearing, then disappearing. She pinched her eyes shut and pressed her small hands against them hard, hoping to blot out the horrific images.

"Oh Mommy," she wailed. "Where are you, Mommy. I need you."

"I'm right here, darling." Her mother's caressing voice floated around her. Olivia's eyes snapped open. Blackness surrounded her. Wildly, her gaze darted about, searching for her mother. "I can't see you, Mommy." She sobbed.

"I'm right behind you, sweetheart."

Olivia spun around.

Her eyes flew open.

Aunt Hattie's contorted face dangled mere inches from hers. Then as quick as a heartbeat, it vanished, leaving behind her sinister laughter swirling in the hollow background, mocking her, and tormenting her until Olivia felt she would go mad at any moment. She yanked air into her starving lungs. Slamming her hands over her ears, she screamed, "Leave me alone!"

The laughter stopped.

The bodies vanished.

Her aunt disappeared.

Her mother's voice ceased.

Olivia was alone.

She lowered herself onto the dank ground and wept. But no one heard her. No one cared.

"We're here." At the sound of Erik's voice, her thoughts were mercifully yanked from that dark abyss of the past and forced back into the present. The soft amber light of the parking lot did little to banish the darkness shrouding her soul. Tears stung the backs of her eyes. Her rapid heartbeat slammed against her ribs. Could Erik hear it? She hoped not. She sat up straight and willed herself to be calm. Years of practice helped her to immediately mask her emotions.

Olivia gazed out the window. She had no recollection of when they had parked. She only knew… Olivia swallowed back the tears constricting her throat as her gaze took in the runways stretched before her.

"I…," Panic seized her. She shook her head. "I can't go in there." Tears filled her voice. Her shoulders slumped and started shaking along with the rest of her body. So much for masking her emotions.

Quick as a flash, Erik unfastened both of their

seatbelts. Olivia felt herself being pulled to his side of the pickup. His strong arms wrapped around her. Not able to contain her tears, the floodgates opened. Olivia sobbed into Erik's shirt. His hands rubbed her back. She allowed him to hold her. No, she needed him to hold her. Without the security of his arms, she might never make it out of the pit of black indelible memories and pain.

As the tears of her vile past continued to flow, Olivia was overwhelmed with gratitude that Erik didn't seek an explanation from her. That he respected her privacy. She loved that about him.

If only she could stay in the comfort of his arms forever. But she knew she had to face the demons of her past. At least she didn't feel like she'd have to do it alone anymore. She had a friend—Erik. She drew back, pulled the hanky Mimi had made for her, and wiped her eyes and nose.

Erik said nothing as he searched her face. Olivia longed for him to pull her into his arms again and kiss away her pain. *Oh, my. Lands o' Goshen! What am I thinking?* Olivia spun her face toward the passenger window. What on earth had come over her? Erik was her boss, and she was thinking about him kissing away her pain? Chalking it up to the insanity of the moment, she was so thankful that Erik couldn't read her mind. He'd be shocked. She knew she was.

Several moments later, reluctantly, Olivia scooted over, reached for the door handle, and froze. The private plane taking off in the distance glued her hand to the handle. Why didn't she let Audra rent a car when she'd offered? Then she wouldn't have to deal with going inside the airport. But, no-o. Olivia insisted she'd be fine. Well, she wasn't. And now she could kick herself. Even Erik couldn't give her the courage she needed to step inside that place. And she definitely wasn't asking God for any either.

♥♥♥

Erik didn't know what to do. Should he ask her what had made her cry and why she seemed so reluctant to go inside, much less to get out of the pickup? *Lord, show me what to do here.*

A moment passed. Then as if the Holy Spirit Himself were talking through him, Erik said, "It's okay, Olivia. I'm here for you. I won't leave you. Whatever it is you're afraid of. Whatever has you so upset, I'm here to help you. *God's* here to help you too."

"God!" she bit out, whirling on him.

The venomous way she said 'God' stunned him so jarringly that he had to force himself not to stare.

Anger coursed across her beautiful face, marring it with hatred. "Where was *God* when my parents' plane went down in the Atlantic Ocean? Where was *God* when my grandma died a few days later? Where was *God* when Hammond's plane crashed? Where was *God* when I was left alone to live with an aunt from Hades who sold my parents' home and left me homeless and penniless? Where was *God* when she gave away all of my parents' things? Don't talk to me about God, Erik!" She yanked on the handle, shoved the door open, and fled toward the airport's entrance.

Erik sat there, staring after her as she disappeared inside. Even if he tried, he doubted he could get his body to move to go after her. He was stunned by what he'd just heard. Stunned that every time she mentioned God, it was laced with venom. He drew in a long breath and slowly let it out. No wonder Olivia always seemed so sad. Losing her parents, her grandmother, her fiancé, her home and her belongings? That would force even the strongest of men to their knees. If her words were any indication, he doubted Olivia bent her knees. Instead she had turned away from the only One Who could truly help her—Father God.

Compassion seized his soul. "That poor woman, Lord." He removed the moisture from the corner of his eyes. "Jesus, have mercy on her. Heal her *everywhere* she hurts. May she come to know You as her comforter, her provider, her savior, and her Lord. Let Your tender mercies flood her life as You surround her with Your love." Erik sighed heavily. Right then and there, he made a pact with himself that if it took him the rest of his life, he would show Olivia God's love. Not with words, but with actions. And he'd start right now.

"Oh, Audra." Olivia hugged her best friend. "It was awful."

"What's wrong?" Audra stepped back and slipped her carry-on bag onto her shoulder. She put her arm around Olivia's shoulder and started walking toward the baggage claim.

Olivia looked at Audra, fighting back the tears. "I've ruined everything. Erik will probably never talk to me again. Especially after the things I said to him. I finally found the job of my dreams and now I'll have to look for another one."

"No, Olivia."

Olivia swung her head toward the sound of Erik's voice. When he had walked along side her, she didn't know. But what she did know was her cheeks were now flaming with humiliation. "I…I'm…" Olivia stuttered.

"You don't have to say anything. And you don't have to look for another job. I want you to stay. You're the best airbrush painter around. I don't want to lose you, Olivia. Or your friendship." Seriousness flowed through his eyes, flooding her with relief. "Besides, real friends are there for each other in good times and in bad."

"Amen, brother. Amen."

Olivia and Erik both yanked their gazes toward Audra.

Audra stepped forward. "Erik. It's a pleasure to meet you." She threw her arms around him, hugging him. "I couldn't have said it better myself."

Olivia watched the exchange until her gaze snagged on a familiar form walking down the concourse amongst several people. Her heart hauled into overdrive. "Hammond!" Olivia squealed. Leaving her friends behind, she took off running toward the place where she'd spotted Hammond.

When Hammond first disappeared, these types of incidences happened to her often, but this one was different. She didn't just think it was him. She knew it *was* him. Olivia rounded the corner, furiously scanning the area, looking for the jacket she'd given him for Christmas the year before. There was no mistaking that jacket. Olivia designed a collage of the things he loved to do and paid a lady to embroider the sketch she'd made onto the back of the coat. Hammond had been wearing it the day he disappeared.

"Olivia. What're you doing?" Audra asked between gulps of air as she stood along side her.

Erik joined them.

Olivia stood on her tiptoes, perusing the crowd. "I saw Hammond."

"Hammond? Oh Livvy. You know he's dead." Audra laced her arm through Olivia's elbow and glanced at Erik.

"He's alive, Audie. I saw him." She didn't miss the exchange between Erik and Audra. They must think she'd lost of all of her brain cells, but she hadn't. She'd seen Hammond. How he knew where she was, and why he ran from her just now, she didn't know. But what she did know was that she was definitely going to find out.

After she had dragged them through every terminal looking for that illusive jacket—the one she never spotted again, they headed back to her cottage. Once there, Olivia turned the key in the lock and reached around the door and flipped the light on. She moved out of the way to let Audra pass.

"Oh, my goodness!" Audra glanced back at her and then back into the house before stepping inside. "This is amazing."

"Isn't it though? I'm so blessed," Olivia stated

although her mind wasn't really on the present.

Audra about gave herself whiplash. "Did I just hear you use the word blessed?"

Olivia shrugged, not really wanting to talk about anything at the moment.

"Where do you want me to put these?" Erik asked from behind her.

Olivia turned and faced him. "I'm sorry, Erik. I forgot about Audra's luggage." She reached out to take them, but Erik shook his head.

"I got 'em." He pulled away from her reach. "Just lead the way, ma'am."

He looked so adorable standing there with a piece of luggage under each arm and one in each hand. Olivia motioned for him to follow her. "This way, sir."

"Sir?" he asked, stepping up beside her. "What's with the sir bit?"

"Well, you called me ma'am. I just thought I would reciprocate with equal formality."

"Ha ha. Very funny."

Olivia flipped the light switch on, and they stepped inside the bedroom. The transition from her old life to her new one was like the giant dip on a roller coaster ride, and the whole exciting adventure made her a touch woozy.

"Oh my goodness!" Audra's gleeful shout from behind them made Olivia jerk. She bolted past them, nearly knocking them both over as she darted inside the bedroom that was to be hers for the next two weeks. "Oh, Liv. This is gorgeous." She ran over to the window and knelt one knee on the burgundy sofa. Shoving the pink and forest green throw pillows out of her way, she inched closer, pressing her chest against the back of the couch. She strained her neck from side to side as she peered out of the floor to ceiling picture window. Two smaller versions of the floor to ceiling windows stood cattycorner next to the large one. "I can't wait to see the view from here in the morning. I bet it's gorgeous." She leapt up and ran to the bed. It too was burgundy with pink and green throw pillows.

For the millionth time, Olivia wondered who designed this house. Each room sported a different style and theme. In this room, the large Victorian-style headboard rounded to a point mere feet away from the ceiling. Surrounding the triangle shape of the headboard were several round glass pictures of women from the Victorian era. The coolest part about this room was the burgundy velvet oval footstool with long fringe at the foot of the bed. Olivia had never seen anything like it before. A wing-backed chair that matched the couch sat at an angle several feet away from the footstool. Yes, Olivia had to admit, she was indeed blessed to be living in such a fine house as this.

"Well, I'd better go."

Olivia spun around. "Oh, Erik. I'm so sorry. It's just that every time I see this room, I can't get over the beauty of it." She tilted her head and looked up at him. "Who decorated this house anyway?"

"Aunt Adell. She loves doing stuff like this. She did my house too. She's a pretty remarkable woman. Talented too."

"I'll say." Audra added.

"Well, I'd better get." Erik turned to leave.

Olivia walked him to the door. He turned to face her. "Erik?"

"Yeah?"

She couldn't look at him, afraid of what she might see in his eyes. "I'm really sorry I broke down like that tonight."

Erik stepped closer to her. "Don't be. That's what friends are for." He gave her a hug and stepped out the door.

The warmth of his hug spread through her, remaining even after he left.

"Just friends, huh?" Audra's meaning came through loud and clear.

Olivia faced her. "Yes. We're just friends." They met at the sofa where they both curled one leg under and sat down. "He was just giving me a neighborly hug is all."

"Oh yeah? From the look on his face, I'd say that that hug was anything but neighborly."

Olivia tilted her head sideways. Her eyes crimped. "What'd'ya mean?" She planted her foot on the couch.

"Well," Audra shifted her body more toward Olivia, her eyes bright and shining with joy. "When he had his arms around you, his eyes were closed and his lips were pursed. It looked as if he never wanted to let you go."

Shocked and confused, Olivia transferred her focus away from Audra. Maybe her best friend read more into his hug than what was there. Then again, ironic as it sounded, she wouldn't really mind if Erik thought of her as more than a friend.

Hammond's face popped in her mind. "Hammond," she whispered.

"Livvy."

Olivia slowly turned toward Audra.

"Did you really see Hammond at the airport?"

"Yes." Her head gave a quick pertinacious nod. "Yes, I did."

Folding her legs Indian style, Audra faced Olivia. "How could it be Hammond? He's dead. You saw the plane. You've seen the police report."

"I don't know." She shook her head. "All I know is I saw him."

"Could it have been Haskell? Maybe he followed me. He's been asking about you a lot lately."

"Nope. There's no way it was Haskell." Her head swayed back and forth.

"How do ya know?"

"Because." She folded her legs in a pretzel shape. Picking up a throw pillow, she laid it on her lap and rested her arms on it as she had done so many times before when a talk with Audra was about to take a serious turn. "Remember the jacket I designed for Hammond? The one Mrs. Marvy embroidered for me?"

Audra nodded.

"Hammond had it on the day he left. The helicopter pilot that lifted his plane off the side of the mountain said there was no body inside the plane or anywhere near Hammond's aircraft."

"Okay." Audra tossed her long black hair over her shoulder. "Let's just say for the sake of saying, that it was

Hammond you saw at the airport and that he did make it out of that plane alive. Why would he run from you? And how did he know where you were in the first place?"

"I don't know." Olivia waved her head from side to side. "I don't know. All I do know is, it was Hammond at the airport."

"If it really was him, what are you going to do? Do you still love him?"

That wasn't as easy to answer as she had always thought it would be. "That's the really bizarre part of all this mess. I'm not sure how I feel about him anymore. When we went to dinner tonight—"

"Wait. We? Who's we?"

"Camara, Chase, Erik and me."

"Who's Camara and Chase?"

"Erik's sister and brother-in-law." Olivia knew she might as well answer Audra or she'd never get through her story. Audra loved details. "Anyway, at the restaurant, this redheaded, gorgeous knock out waited on us. Erik never even batted an eyelash her direction. Remember how Hammond used to flirt with every beautiful woman he came in contact with?"

Audra nodded, having been there for the performance more than once.

"That used to hurt me terribly. But," she sighed. "I was so afraid if I said something that I would lose him." She looked down at the pillow and ran her fingers over the soft fabric as mega doses of Hammond's imperfections blazed through her mind. "Really, Audra. I had placed Hammond on such a pedestal. As far as I was concerned he could do no wrong. But the more I think about things, the more I realize that Hammond wasn't the Prince Charming I made him out to be. To be honest, sometimes he acted more like a toad instead of a prince."

Audra's eyelids bolted open. "Wow. Coming from you, that's a shocker. You used to think Hammond hung the moon."

"I did. But the more I've thought about things, the more I realized that while most of the time he was a real sweetheart, there were times when he could be pretty controlling and demanding. Like when I first met him at Blackwater Falls. He wouldn't take no for an answer and insisted on my having dinner with him even though I made it clear that I already had plans with you."

"And yet you loved him." Audra's comment was a statement, not a question.

"I did." She tossed the pillow aside. "I was in love with his adventurous spirit. I went places and did things I'd never done before. His love for me gave me a reason to go on. So, in my eyes, that made him some kind of hero. Even his controlling ways I treasured to a degree because he took charge of things when I wasn't able to." A wistful sigh escaped. "I just wished he loved me enough to not fly that day."

"So, now what? What if it is Hammond, and he's come to take you back?"

"I don't know." Her shoulders hiked, and her head jerked in short choppy movements. "I wish I knew the answer to that question."

"Do you still love him?" Audra asked her again.

Olivia sucked one side of her bottom lip in. She was no closer to answering that question than she was just moments ago. But knowing her friend wouldn't back off until she did, she turned her face toward the window, contemplating how to answer her friend satisfactorily. Seconds ticked by until finally, she drew in a long breath and plunged forward with the best answer she had right now. "I'm not sure, Audie. Every time I think of what he put poor Haskell and his parents through. What he put *me* through…." The familiar ache of losing him pressed into her heart. "I still can't believe he went ahead and flew even after I begged him not to, and even after they warned him repeatedly not to go because of the huge risk involved. But then again," she sighed heavily. "It's my fault he did."

Olivia's gaze snagged on the silhouette of a man standing outside her living room window. She sucked in a sharp breath and let out a scream loud enough to resurrect the dead.

Chapter Twelve

"Olivia!" Erik yelled, pounding on her door.

Terror spread through Olivia. Another scream escaped. Her wild eyes darted back and forth between the window and the door. The person who'd been standing at her window had vanished. She leapt up from the couch and darted toward the door. Certain her heart would come out of her chest at any moment, she turned the lock and swung it open. Olivia thrust herself into Erik's chest, nearly sending both of them backward. Audra's carry-on bag flew out of his hand and across the floor. His arms immediately wrapped around her, holding her tight, and she clung to him for dear life.

Within seconds, Audra was at her side. "What's the matter? What's going on?"

Not really wanting to, Olivia loosened her hold on Erik, but fear compelled her to not let go of him completely. She needed the security his strong arms provided. Removing one arm from around his waist, she pointed toward the living room window. "I," she swallowed down the clump of fright sticking in her throat. "I saw a man standing out there."

Erik gently removed her arm from around him, then sprinted toward the window. He looked both ways before returning to where Olivia stood glued to the spot. "Stay here. I'll be back. I'm going to check outside."

"No!" Olivia yanked on his arm.

Erik looked down at her. Prying her fingers off is arm, his face hardened with concern. "It'll be okay. I'll be careful." With that he stepped outside the opened door and into the darkness.

Olivia looped elbows with Audra. What she really wanted to do was run after Erik, but fear firmly cemented her in place. What if something happened to Erik too? Would she lose yet another loved one?

Loved one?

The realization that she loved him slammed into her like a fist to the gut. "No," she whimpered. "No."

"What's wrong?" Alarm rang through Audra's voice.

"I can't. I just can't."

"You can't what?" Audra tugged on Olivia's chin until her eyes met hers. "Liv, what are you talking about?"

Tears pooled in her eyes. "I—I love Erik."

When Erik arrived at the front door of Olivia's cottage, he couldn't believe his ears. Olivia loved him? That revelation revved up his heart several rpms.

"I can't love him, Audie. I just can't."

Those same raised rpms seized like a frozen engine block. Why? he wanted to ask, but if she knew he was listening, she'd probably freak.

"Everyone I've ever loved, died."

"Oh, thanks. So you're saying you don't love me?"

Audra asked, clearly trying to lighten the moment.

"You know what I mean." Frustration pushed through her voice.

"No, I don't. You keep saying that, but I'm still here. And I've been here for over twenty years. Livvy, you've got to let go of the past. You have to take a chance. Erik seems like a wonderful guy. Don't throw a chance at real love away."

Yeah. Listen to the woman, Olivia. He heard a weird sort of nervous chuckle.

"Well, I guess I don't really have to worry about that. He sees me as just a friend. At first, that's all I wanted. But, now. I'm not so sure. Oh, Audie. All of this is so confusing. How can a person fall in love with someone in just three weeks? Especially someone like me who's sworn never to love anyone again." Olivia blew out a puffy breath while shaking her head furiously. "Besides Erik is my boss. And I refuse to jeopardize what I have here for something that makes absolutely no sense. Loving Erik is simply out of the question. That's all there is too it."

Erik decided that was his cue to enter. Only he needed to give them advanced notice of his arrival so as not to frighten them further. "Olivia." He stepped into the house. She whirled, and all color fled from her face. As hard as it was not to react to what she'd said, he didn't want to embarrass her. "I searched the grounds and didn't see anyone." Not wanting to scare her further, he deliberately left out his findings.

She rubbed her eyes. "This has been a long, emotional day. Maybe I just imagined seeing someone."

It wasn't her imagination, but Erik refused to upset her further by telling her that. After he'd grabbed a flashlight out of his truck, he'd gone around back. He followed a set of large footprints around the house and into the wooded area. Whoever Olivia saw had fled.

♥♥♥

Much to her dismay, Olivia' insides were still trembling. When she told them it must have been her imagination, she knew it hadn't been. Someone had definitely been outside her window. She cut a glance at Erik. His presence helped ease her trembling insides and her fear.

"Would y'all like a cup of coffee? Or some ice-cold lemonade?" she offered, not wanting Erik to leave.

One of his eyebrows spiked, and he studied her as if he were contemplating what to do. "If you're not too tired, I'd love a glass of lemonade."

Some of the knots in her stomach unraveled. "No, it's not too late."

"I'd love some too," Audra piped in. "But, hey, why don't y'all go sit down and let me get it?"

Bless her heart. Olivia knew what her friend was up to. They'd lived together long enough that Audra knew when Olivia was still scared. But still, Audie was her guest, and Olivia wanted to wait on her. "Thanks for the offer. But I can get it. Besides, you don't even know where the glasses are."

Audra tsked. "Well, duh. How hard can it be?" She smiled, her eyes twinkling with mirth. "There are only so many cupboards in a kitchen. And I'm assuming the lemonade is in the fridge, and the ice is in the icebox. And if it isn't, then you've got one whale of a water puddle somewhere." Audra laughed, obviously pleased with herself. "Please, Liv. Let me do this. I'd feel better if you went and sat down."

Olivia couldn't refuse the pleading look in her eyes. Besides, her knees were still weak from the ordeal. She nodded. "Thank you."

Audra smiled, then bolted toward the kitchen.

Olivia looked over at Erik. "Would you like to sit down?"

"Sounds good." Erik took her elbow and led her toward the sofa.

An hour and half breezed by, and the fear had finally subsided. Erik offered to stay and sleep on the couch, but Olivia declined his kind offer, convincing him that she was fine now and that Audra was here with her. Reluctantly he left with the promise that they would call him if they needed him. Exhausted from the stressful ordeals of the day, Olivia fell into bed.

The next morning, at Erik's arena, Olivia breathed in the tepid morning air filled with fuel, grease, dirt, coffee, and something sweet. Men, women, and children milled about getting autographs and snapping pictures of themselves next to the monster trucks and their drivers.

As Olivia and Audra wove their way through the maze of monster trucks to get to Erik's, Olivia felt like a dwarf amongst all the mammoth vehicles. They strolled up to the Mad Masher.

"Oh, Livvy! This is your best one ever." Audra stood back, admiring Olivia's masterpiece. "I love those eyes. He looks like he's fixin' to take a chunk out of those cars."

"She did a fabulous job, didn't she?" The admiration in Erik's eyes was worth all of the hard work she'd put into this project. "I think I'll keep her around."

Something about the way he looked at her and the way he said he'd 'keep her around' made her wonder if his words held a double connotation. *Oh, please, Olivia. Get a grip. Just because you think you love him doesn't mean he feels that way about you. Anyway, you need to nip those feelings in the bud. It's not going anywhere and you know it.*

"Well, I'm up next. I'd better get ready."

Olivia watched Erik put on his fire gear and guzzle a bottle of Gatorade. Audra and Olivia stepped back when he ducked underneath the fiberglass body and climbed up inside the Mad Masher. When he fired up the truck, Audra's hands flew to her ears. Not Olivia. She loved hearing the monster truck's massive roar. Olivia grabbed Audra's hand and tugged her forward. "C'mon. Let's grab a seat in the stands so we can watch him."

They ran to the grandstands and climbed several stairs. "Where ya going?" Audra puffed. "What's wrong with the seats down below?"

"I want to get up high enough so I can see him."

They sat on the dark blue wooden bench. Olivia leaned forward, waiting for the announcer to call Erik's name. From where she sat, she could see Erik's truck on the left entrance, and a big black monster truck on the right.

"Coming up next is Erik Cole in the Mad Masher. He's one of the tough ones to beat today. Along with Brody Taylor in the Extreme-a-nator."

Cheers rose from the crowd. A young man stood up in front of Olivia.

"Hey, sit down!" she yelled, shocking both him and herself.

His mother pulled him down. "Sorry."

Olivia sent her a polite smile and returned her attention to the race just in time to see both monster trucks come speeding down the arena.

"Here they come now racing down thunder alley folks, over sixty miles an hour," the announcer yelled, his voice blazing with excitement. "Into the turn," he continued as Olivia watched them slow down and make a sharp turn. "O-o-h this looks pretty even," the man continued.

The left front and back wheel on Erik's truck raised off the ground about a foot. Olivia clutched the seat and held back a scream. Her hands relaxed the second Erik righted the massive beast. The loud roar of the trucks when they hammered it, as Erik called it, sent goose bumps racing up and down Olivia's spine. In eager anticipation, she gripped the bleacher chair with her hands, cutting off the circulation in them. Both drivers, now neck-and-neck, hit a dirt ramp.

"This is close folks."

It sure is, Olivia agreed with the loudspeaker. Every muscle in her body tensed with excitement.

Their trucks flew, noses first, up into the air, a good twenty feet or more.

Olivia fought the urge to stand, especially after she'd just yelled at the boy in front of her for doing that very same thing. Chills raced up and down her spine as her adrenaline shifted into high gear. She held her breath as she watched Erik's truck lunge over the finish line. The front wheels hit seconds before the rear wheels. A couple of short bounces and it was over. Olivia jumped to her feet, clapping her approval.

"What a race!" The voice over the loud speaker bellowed. "Brody Taylor won, but not by much."

Olivia tuned out the announcer and grabbed her friend's hand, yanking her up. "C'mon, Audra." They hurried down the steps and ran toward the contestants' pit, carefully making their way to where Erik had parked.

Erik climbed out, removed his helmet and gloves, and slid out of the fireproof suit. Ben stepped up and handed him another Gatorade. While Erik guzzled the drink, Olivia noticed Ben looking at her. Instead of his usual friendly manner, his eyes were glazed with animosity. Erik must have talked to him about stopping by to see her every morning. After that day Erik showed up and Ben looked uncomfortable, Ben hadn't been back. But she had no idea it would make him this angry.

The way he continued to glare at her made her nervous. She tore her gaze from him and put it on Erik. "Wow. You must have been thirsty." She stepped closer to him.

"I have to drink a lot before and after driving. Because of the fire suit you can get dehydrated really fast. That's probably our biggest concern. Trust me, getting dehydrated is no fun."

"Hey, bubba!" Camara threw herself at her brother. He picked her up and swung her around before planting her back on the ground. "Great job! Nice save back there."

Chase grabbed Erik's hand, then pulled him into a hug. "Pretty fancy drivin'."

"Not good enough. Brody beat me."

"Well, you can get him in the freestyle." Camara's voice oozed with confidence.

Chase and Camara turned toward Olivia.

"Good to see you again," Camara said.

"You too."

Camara's gaze shifted toward Audra.

"Where are my manners? Camara, this is Audra, Audra this is Camara."

"Nice to meet you." They met in the middle of the little group and shook hands.

Camara stepped back beside Chase. "This is my husband Chase."

Audra shook Chase's hand. "Nice to meet you."

"Likewise." Chase nodded.

Olivia's hungry stomach chose that moment to growl. She looked around to see if anyone else had heard it. Much to her relief, no one seemed to notice it because of all the noise around them. "How long until the next event?"

"They'll start in about an hour. They're bringing in some cars and stuff now." Erik turned toward the workers who were unloading a bright red, giant storage container.

In fear of her perpetually growling stomach, Olivia anchored her arms across her middle. "Well, I'm going to go find something to eat. I'm famished."

"Me, too," Erik, Audra, Camara, and Chase all said.

Everyone laughed.

"You can't be too hungry yet." Erik's teasing voice yanked her attention his direction.

"Oh yeah?" She planted her hands on her hips. "And why is that?"

"Cuz I haven't heard that stomach of yours roar yet."

Whether it was guilt or embarrassment, Olivia wasn't sure, but heat rushed into her cheeks.

"Ah ha. I knew it." He looked so pleased with himself. "It did rumble. You just lucked out. With all of the noise around here, none of us heard it."

"That's a first," she mumbled under her breath. Why did she have to have a stomach that alerted the whole world to her hunger? It was down right embarrassing. She should be used to it by now, but she wasn't. Avoiding direct eye contact with anyone, she said, "Audra and I are going to the concession stand. You want us to bring anything back? Or did y'all want to go with us?"

"I need to check some things here." Erik nodded his head toward the Mad Masher. His pit crew was already wrenching on the truck. She learned that term from Erik. It just meant working on it, but the monster truck drivers couldn't be that ordinary about anything. "Would you mind bringing me something back?" he asked.

"Of course I don't mind. I'm happy to do it." Olivia felt her lips curl upward.

Erik stuck his hand inside the pocket of his jeans and pulled out a money clip. "I'd like a couple of foot long chili-cheese dogs and a large, fresh-squeezed lemonade." He removed the clip, peeled off two bills, and handed her two twenties.

Olivia stared at the money. "Dogs cost that much?" She gasped, looking at him.

"No, I want to treat everyone to lunch."

"I can get mine," Olivia said quickly.

"I know you *can*, but I wanna buy. Please?" His dipped chin, sad puppy dog eyes, and protruding lips tempted her to want to kiss him. Disgusted with herself for getting carried away with her emotions, she stopped herself from rolling her eyes at herself and her wondering imagination.

"Okay. What does everyone want?" She looked at Audra. "Help me keep all of this straight."

"I'll go, too, if y'all don't mind." Camara stepped closer to them.

"No, not at all." It blessed Olivia that Camara wanted to go with them. *There's that word blessed again. Ugh.* She needed to get him and his comments out of her head, or her heart wasn't going to have any chance at all.

After taking their orders, the three of them made their way to the long concession stand line where they chatted like they'd known each other forever. Olivia really liked Camara. In fact, she'd love to have her for a sister. *Ack! Stop this nonsense. I don't want to love anyone—not now, not ever.* So why was she allowing such ridiculous thoughts to even enter her mind?

"Don't you think so, Livvy?"

Olivia blinked. *Didn't she think so what?* What had

she missed this time?

"Were you daydreaming again, girlfriend?" Audra looped elbows.

Olivia knew her flushed cheeks were giving her away.

Audra tucked her chin to her neck and peered up at her.

"Okay, okay. Yes, I was daydreaming again. So there. Are you happy now?" Olivia feigned aggravation.

"What were ya dreamin' about?" Camara asked. She stuck the tip of her straw in her mouth and took a drink, never taking her eyes off of Olivia as they headed back.

Olivia's face flamed. No way would she tell Camara what she was thinking. She could just see it now. *Oh yeah, by the way. I'm in love with your brother and I want you for a sister-in-law. Lands o' Goshen. That would certainly go over big.*

The toe of Olivia's shoe snagged on a clump of dirt. Instinctively, she hoisted the food carriers upward. They teetered precariously as she scrambled to maintain her balance.

"Oh, Livvy! Are you okay?" Audra reached to right her.

With lightning quickness, she regained control of her body. "Is that all anyone can ever say to me?" She chuckled nervously.

"What do you mean?" Camara questioned her. Her big brown eyes, so like Erik's, focused on Olivia's face.

"Oh nothing." She bobbled her head. "It's just that I'm forever finding myself in a pickle."

"Ooo. I know that one. Me, too." Camara giggled, then

puffed her bangs out of the way.

It was then that Olivia noticed the scar above Camara's eye. "Erik told me that you nearly died. Do you mind if I ask what happened?"

"No, not at all. I was checking under the hood of The Black Beast." At the hike of Olivia's eyebrows, Camara said, "The Black Beast was my bog truck."

"Oh." She nodded.

"Someone had messed with the NOS, and I didn't know it. So, when Erik fired up my bogger, everything blew. I don't remember much about it, only that I woke up in the hospital with a huge headache and some pretty painful burns and nasty cuts on my arms. It could have been worse. A piece of metal could have gone through my skull, and I would have been a goner. But God didn't let that happen. Hey, speaking of God… Would y'all like to go to church with us tomorrow?"

"We'd love to," Audra piped in before Olivia could respond.

Olivia nearly twisted her neck off and almost sent the food flying onto the ground again when she spun and glared at her friend. "Uh, I have other plans."

Audra didn't miss a beat. "What other plans?"

Pursing her lips and narrowing her eyes, Olivia made sure she sent a silent message to her friend to knock it off.

Audra just smiled and said, "Whatever they are, you can change them." She turned toward Camara. "Just name the time and place and we'll be there."

What was up with Audra? She had never done that to Olivia before. She always respected her wish to not attend church. How could she do that to her knowing she never wanted to step foot inside any church again? Just wait until she got her hands on her. Olivia's insides boiled over. *Tomorrow ought to be a real hoot. Not!*

♥♥♥

"What's the difference between the freestyle and timed event?" Olivia asked. Never taking her eyes off of Erik, she bit into her chili-cheese covered corn dog and waited for his answer.

Erik set his chili-cheese hot dog down and finished chewing. Drink in hand, he took a long pull before answering her. "The timed-event is what you just watched. We race down thunder alley into the arena, make a hook, which is a quick U-turn, and then race back to jump over a ramp. The best time, which averages about seventeen seconds, usually wins. Freestyle is a judged event. Whatever you can do in two minutes to get the fans excited gets you more points."

"What gets them exited?" Audra asked before Olivia had a chance.

"Cyclones, leaping over huge things in a row like semi-trailers, mobile homes, and delivery trucks. Like the way I have it set up here." He pointed toward the arena, and Olivia's gaze followed. "You can't really tell from here, but I have things butted together. One of the obstacles has a single car, then two stacked cars right next to it, then a delivery truck, and then a semi-trailer."

The whites of Olivia's eyes showed. She couldn't

imagine leaping over something that big.

"The record for the longest jump is 202 feet over a 747 airplane. The crowd goes wild when you clear stuff like that, or you walk your truck. I hate to say it, but your ego really gets stroked when the fans are on their feet, rooting for ya. In fact, there's even a saying amongst us monster truck drivers that our egos are as big as our trucks. But not mine." He chuckled. His eyes rolled, his mouth quirked, and he shook his head.

They all laughed with him.

"Is there anything else you can do to get a higher score?" Olivia leaned forward, waiting for his answer.

"Well, ya wanna avoid wrecks if ya can. A good save is great for points. And the more air you get, the higher the score."

"More air?" Olivia cocked her head sideways. "You also mentioned walking your truck. What's that?"

"More air is the higher your truck leaps in the air, the better. Walking your truck is when it's vertical on two wheels only." Erik crunched his trash together. "Pogoing gets the crowd going too."

"Pogoing?" Olivia wanted to know what that meant too.

"Yeah, it's like popping a wheelie and landing on your tailgate. Well," Erik stood. "As much as I hate to cut this short, I'd better get or I'll miss my turn."

"Wouldn't want that," Olivia said, hoping her nerves could stand watching his turn. Especially after all that talk about walking his truck, pogoing it, and leaping in the air.

Minutes later, Olivia and Audra were seated in the

stands. The voice over the loudspeaker announcing that Erik was up next made the hair on Olivia's arms rise.

"Get ready to hear some horsepower folks." The announcer's voice blasted around them. "Here comes Erik Cole barreling down thunder alley."

The moment she saw Erik's truck enter the arena as if his backside was on fire, she sat on the edge of the seat. Every muscle in her body tensed.

When Erik slowed down around a corner, the monster truck body dipped slightly forward. When he accelerated, it tilted backward. Olivia pulled two pieces of gum out of her pocket and chewed rapidly as he headed toward a row of cars. Right before he hit the first one, she heard him let off the accelerator and then hit it again when his front tires leapt in the air. Olivia couldn't believe how high up he was when he cleared them.

"Wow! Talk about sick air folks," the announcer's excited voice blared through the speakers.

The crowd leaped to their feet.

Olivia could feel the energy radiating from them. She scanned the crowd. People waved Mad Masher banners, checkered flags, and homemade signs that read: Go Mad Masher. Erik Cole Rocks!

After jumping over a mobile home and several ramps, Erik did what he called a cyclone. Like a top spinning in place, around and around the Mad Masher went, kicking up dust. The crowd roared while Olivia held her breath, fearful that he would flip over. Just when she thought it was safe to breathe, he stopped the cyclone and walked the Mad Masher over a storage container that didn't crush. Seeing the giant truck at a vertical angle, not only sucked out what little breath she had left, but caused her heart to pick up even more momentum.

Back on four wheels, Erik drove his truck toward the obstacle with the semi-trailer. This time, her heart stopped beating altogether when he hit the first car and the front end shot up in the air. He leapt over the vehicles and the semi-trailer. His front tires hit first and then the back. Immediately he went into another cyclone. Again the crowd rose to their feet, hollering and whistling until Olivia thought her eardrums would burst. Olivia's heart whirled with him as she watched him go around and around and around. It looked like at any moment his tire might grab and he would flip over.

Olivia hoped his two minutes were almost up. She didn't know how much more she could take.

Then Erik headed toward what looked like a rail car with some smashed cars in front of it. Up and over it he flew.

"O-oh! Now, that's some air! The fans are lovin' it!" The deep voice rattled off something else, but Olivia couldn't hear him over the roar of the crowd.

Next Erik leapt over a hill close to where she was sitting. He picked up momentum and soared over a second hill. The Mad Masher went vertical, then the rear frame slammed into the ground, sending big pieces of the fiberglass-body flying before it flipped over and landed on its top. "Erik!" Olivia screamed, jumping up.

Fear clutched her as she watched three men rush toward him. Seeing his truck laying upside down, Olivia just knew he had to be hurt… or worse…

Audra put her arm around her shoulder. “He’ll be fine.”

She wanted to believe her best friend, but her past record with loved ones didn’t leave her with much hope.

Erik climbed out the window, removed his helmet, and waved to the crowd. Tears of relief poured from her eyes as Erik’s gaze snagged on hers. But his smile did nothing to stop the fear or the pounding of her heart.

Olivia and Audra made their way to the pits as fast as their legs would carry them. When she saw Erik heading toward her, she suddenly felt shy and embarrassed. What would he think about her crying? Within seconds, his rock-solid arms pulled her to his chest. “Hey, my friend, it’s okay.” He laid his hand on the back of her head and pressed it closer to his chest. “The roll cages are built sturdy enough to take that kind of abuse. Besides, I’m strapped in there so tight that I don’t even budge. This stuff happens all the time.”

Those words that were meant to comfort her barreled into her. Great. Someone else Olivia loved lived dangerously. Good thing he called her friend because at the moment he’d said that happens all the time, she decided to never allow herself to give into the love she felt for him. Never.

♥♥♥

Sunday morning, Olivia leaned over her bathroom vanity and finished putting her makeup on. She still couldn’t believe she was going to church. And not just with Audra, but with Erik, Chase, and Camara too. There was no way she felt she could back out gracefully.

"Livvy." Audra knocked on her bathroom door. "You ready?"

She should be mad at Audra for agreeing that they would go to church, but she couldn't. Audra loved her and only wanted what was best for her. The only problem was that God wasn't what was best for her. That Olivia knew for certain.

"Livvy," she sing-songed. "Erik's here to pick us up. C'mon."

That was another thing Audra had talked her into. She'd wanted to take her car, but when Erik offered to taxi everyone there, Audra had agreed without consulting Olivia first. She couldn't believe her friend's boldness when she asked Erik if he would mind taking them to Tamarack food court to try out that Fried Green Tomato sandwich he'd bragged about the other night when they were all sitting around chatting. And her audacity didn't stop there. Audra proceeded to ask him if they could do some shopping while there. Olivia had wanted to slide under the table and slink away, but Erik didn't seem to mind. Actually, now that she thought about it, he seemed rather pleased.

Because Olivia had heard such fabulous reviews about that place and she couldn't wait to see it, she didn't fight the issue. Against her better judgment, of course.

"Coming." She quickly rubbed some coral gloss on her lips and pushed away from the sink before opening the door. "I'm ready."

"Wow. You look nice. Where'd you get the pretty blue dress?" Audra's gaze went all the way to the floor. "Oh, and matching shoes too? Wow. Who are we trying to impress?"

Not taking the bait, Olivia pushed past her and headed down the hallway. "Friday was payday. Erik gave me the day off, so in the morning I drove to Charleston Town Center Mall and picked it up."

"You?" Audra dipped her head sideways. "Miss, I-can't-find-my-way-around-my-own-block-without-getting-lost you?"

Olivia laughed at the skepticism dancing in Audra's eyes. "Yes. Me. I used the computer at the shop and printed off a map. You'd really be proud of me. I only got lost twice."

"Only twice, huh? That is an improvement." They laughed and headed toward the door.

Olivia stuffed her house key, a package of gum, and her coin purse in the hidden pockets of her dress. She grabbed a light blue sweater off the coat rack by the door and stepped outside. The early morning sun hadn't yet warmed up the outdoors, so Olivia slid her arms into her sweater, relishing its warmth.

"Morning, Erik." Olivia reeled in her skyrocketing emotions upon seeing him.

"Good morning, ladies. Your chariot awaits." He bowed and made a sweeping motion toward his truck.

"What a nut," Audra commented for Olivia's ears only. "Good morning, kind sir." Audra imitated a British accent, then curtsied.

Olivia slanted a sideways glance at her crazy friend and smiled. “Speaking of nuts.”

“What’s that about nuts?” Erik asked.

“Nothing. Nothing at all.” Audra perkily replied.

Olivia rolled her eyes and shook her head at Miss Bubbly. “I said my friend is nuts.”

Erik looked at the two of them and nodded before opening the passenger door for them. Audra stood on her tiptoes and peered inside the backseat. “Where’s Chase and Camara?”

“They wanted to take their own vehicle.”

“Oh, well, then I can sit in back. That way it won’t be so crowded up front.” With her back to Erik, Olivia gave Audra the ol’ evil eye.

Erik didn’t argue, which made Olivia uneasy. For the sake of her heart, she didn’t want to be up front with him or anywhere else with him right now. She already struggled with keeping her wits about her where he was concerned. Well, at least Audra didn’t insist that all three of them sit up front. For that she was truly grateful, because Audra would have made sure Olivia was seated next to Erik. That would have really been awkward and extremely dangerous on Olivia’s heart. She realized that she was staring at him. With a quick yank, she pulled her focus away from his neatly pressed black denim jeans that hugged his muscular legs and light blue polo shirt that emphasized his broad shoulders and trim waist. Being attracted to this man or being in love with him was the last thing she needed… or wanted. Ugh. It was so easy to keep telling herself that, and so very hard to remember in his presence.

While he helped Audra into his truck, Olivia noticed for the first time that he had running boards. Strange. That first time she'd ridden with him, he had hoisted her up into his truck when she could have used the step. That thought was too confusing to dwell on, so she pushed it away.

She raised her leg to place her foot on the running board when Erik's voice vibrated behind her, "You know, blue's my favorite color. You look great." Between the man's masculine voice, his anise scented warm breath brushing against her ear, and the emotions they evoked in her, Olivia missed the step. Erik's hand tightened around her elbow to keep her from falling face forward.

"You okay?"

"There's those words again." She giggled to cover up her embarrassment. "I'm fine."

"That's for sure."

She stiffened. What did he mean by that? Whatever it was, she didn't want to know. After he made sure she was seated and he shut the door, she wondered if she'd heard him correctly. Did he say she sure was fine?

"So that's why you bought blue. It's Erik's favorite color," Audra chided from the backseat.

Olivia swung her body sideways toward Audra. "Be quiet. He might hear you," she rebuked her in a stage whisper.

"O-o-o-h-h-h. So, you *did* buy blue because of him then."

"That's not what I meant and you know it." She narrowed her eyes. Desperately, she wanted to reach back and slap Audra into next week.

"Oh, yeah. Since when do you buy blue dresses?" Audra placed her fingertip on her lips. "Uh, try never. Not as long as I've known you anyway."

Olivia opened her mouth to retaliate, but the driver side door opened, and Erik hopped in.

"You ready, ladies?" He grabbed his seatbelt, latched it, and then started the truck.

"We sure are. Aren't we, Livvy?"

Again Olivia sent Audra a you're-cruising-for-a-bruising look. Her best friend winked and smiled at her. Olivia pressed her back against the seat, locked her focus heavenward, and thought, *it's gonna to be a long, long day.*

Chapter Thirteen

The brick church with the white window shutters and a white cross on top looked isolated amidst a forest of trees. As they headed toward the French doors, a middle-aged couple toting six children behind them greeted them. The closer they got to the building, the more Olivia's insides trembled. As discreetly as possible, she stuck her hand in her pocket and fiddled with her gum until she popped two little rectangle pieces out. She faked a cough so she could cover her mouth to hide popping the gum inside, then slowly started chewing the breathy peppermint.

"Nervous are we?"

She glared at her friend. If Audra kept this up, Olivia was either going to box her ears or send her packing.

When they stepped inside, an elderly gentleman shook each of their hands, welcoming them. He grabbed Erik and hugged him. "Good ta see ya agin, son."

"Good to see you too, Mr. Mortimer. How are you?"

"I'm a feelin' right pert today. 'specially aftur readin' me them thar obituaries in the mornin' paper and seen my name weren't in it." He cackled. "Well, son. Iffen y'all wanna a seat, ya best be for goin' an a sittin' down. This place is fillin' up mighty fast."

"Thank you, sir."

Without asking what either one of them thought,

Olivia quickly slid into the back pew. She placed her legs off to the side, hoping Erik and Audra would get the hint that she wanted to sit on the outside. That way if it got too uncomfortable, she could make her getaway. Ugh. Just what had she been thinking by coming here, anyway? Must be a case of temporary insanity. There was no other plausible explanation for it.

Audra quickly stepped past her and went one more seat down, leaving Erik to sit next to her. Olivia dipped her brows and pursed her lips at Audra. That gal was really asking for it. But before she could think of a suitably horrible torture to get even with her friend, music filled the sanctuary. Erik squeezed by and lowered himself beside her. Their row filled up fast.

Seconds later, Camara, Chase, and Adell arrived, waved, and pointed up front.

The worship leader asked everyone to stand and worship the Lord. Not caring what anyone thought, Olivia remained seated, arms anchored over her chest. She refused to be a hypocrite. There was no way she was going to worship a God who had abandoned her.

Several songs later, the worship leader strummed his guitar, his soft voice drifted over the church as he spoke. "Do you feel abandoned by God?"

Like the hard pew underneath her, Olivia stiffened. Without turning her neck, her eyes darted wildly around the room, wondering who had ratted her out. Audra was the only one who knew exactly how she felt. Somehow Audra must have managed to talk to that man and told him. She wanted to look at Audra to see if she could detect any form of guilt on her face, but she didn't want anyone to see the shock on hers.

"Has something tragic caused you to feel like God doesn't care one iota about you or your life?"

Okay, this was getting freaky. Olivia furiously attacked her chewing gum until her jaw started to ache.

"Did you turn to God during those tragic times? Or, did you turn away from God?"

Olivia's gaze darted toward the door. One more question like that, and she didn't care what anyone thought, she would be out of here.

Erik's hand slipped under hers. His fingers curled around hers. She swung her head toward him and stared into his face. Was he in on this? What was happening here? Had he told them? Again her gaze flew to the door. It was looking better and better with each passing second.

Gently, Erik squeezed her hand. She slowly looked at him again, hoping her heart didn't show everything she was thinking.

"It's okay, Livvy," he whispered.

Livvy? Did he just call her Livvy? She squirmed in her seat.

"So many times when bad things happen," the man playing the guitar started to talk again. "We want to blame someone. So we end up blaming God. But let me tell y'all. The devil is a deceiver. If he can somehow get you to believing that God is your enemy, then he has succeeded in what he set out to do. And that is, to destroy your relationship with Christ."

Is that what she'd been doing? Listening to the lies of

the devil? Had he deceived her into believing God was her enemy? Olivia closed her eyes. She didn't know what to think anymore. After all, God could have prevented her loved ones' deaths, but He didn't. And what kind of a loving God allows a small child to be left to the mercy of a wicked aunt? Fresh anger assaulted her as she realized the devil hadn't deceived her. The facts were, God had let them die, and then He sent her to live with an aunt from Hades, totally disregarding her prayers. No, God was definitely to blame.

"If that's you, I challenge you to give those things to Him today as we continue to worship Him. Ask Him to heal those hurts. He is the only One who can."

Olivia pulled her hand from Erik's and crossed her arms. Yeah right. Like God would listen to her. He hadn't before, so what made that man think He would listen to her today. She glanced around the room. These people were the ones who were deceived. They believed in a God Who cared about them. A God Who would heal their hurts. Well, could God bring back her loved ones? No. Had He ever cared about what she wanted? No. Not one little bit. And she didn't care who tried to tell her differently. They were wrong. She had the broken, destitute heart to prove it.

After the worship was over, a man wearing a neatly pressed shirt and slacks walked up to the podium.

"I was thinking about what Bruce said today." He glanced at the worship leader and then back toward the congregation. "When my wife and my four children died…"

Olivia's chin jerked upward, and her attention collided

onto the pastor.

"I knew I couldn't make it without God's help. I needed Him."

Why? she wanted to scream.

"Someone asked me one day. Why are you still serving God after he killed your family?"

Olivia wanted to know the answer to that one too.

"First of all, God didn't *kill* my family. An inexperienced driver on icy roads caused the accident that took them. Not God."

Yeah, but He could have prevented it.

"To be honest, I don't have all the answers as to why this happened. All I know is, I'm grateful that when tragedy struck, my foundation in Christ was solid. My relationship with Him wasn't based on what He did or didn't do for me. It was based on a loving, trusting relationship no matter what."

That's a loving relationship? Killing your wife and children? Bitterness churned inside her, rising to the surface of her soul faster than a spewing geyser. *Well, buddy, you can have it.*

"I can't even count the number of times I reread the story of Joseph. Talk about someone who understood suffering. His own brothers sold him into slavery. One tragedy after another happened to him. But in all that time, he never once cursed God. He clung to God. His hope was in his God. He knew God would see him through every vile thing he was going through. In fact." He opened his Bible and rustled some pages. "In Genesis chapter fifty, verse twenty, Joseph told his brothers, 'But as for you, you meant evil against me; but God meant it for good.'"

Whoa. Another déjà vu thing. Without turning her head, she looked at Erik. Just recently, he'd said something very similar to her. Someone had to have told this man just what she'd been going through, and she wanted to know who it was. Anger snapped over the anger already there. Someone was going to answer for putting her in this unbearable, totally awkward position.

"In the midst of my tragedy, I clung to that scripture. Like Joseph, I knew something good would eventually come from the worst time in my life. One good thing that came from it was I experienced God's sustaining power."

Oh yeah? Where was His sustaining power when my loved ones died?

"During my grieving process, the more I turned to God, the more I learned about entering into His rest, His peace. Continually, I cried out to God to keep me from doing what Hebrews chapter three, verse twelve says, 'Beware, brethren, lest there be in any of you an evil heart of unbelief in departing from the living God.' It would have been so easy for me to run away from God instead of to Him. After all, I couldn't understand how he could allow my family to be killed, especially when it was my daily habit to pray for their protection. Except for that day."

Well, she had prayed for Hammond's protection, and he still died. So obviously even doing it right didn't guarantee God's favor.

"I beat myself up for the longest time. I even started to shun God. Then one day a dear friend showed me that it was my guilt that was keeping me from running to God."

A chink fell out of the self-erected fortress wall she'd spent years building. The one that shielded her heart from any further hurt. Had her guilt in killing her parents kept her from turning to God?

"My friend encouraged me to cast the care of that guilt over onto the Lord. At first it was hard. I felt I deserved to suffer because I hadn't prayed that day. But each time the devil reminded me of that fact, I knew I had to make a choice. We all do. We can either turn to God or turn away from Him. Praise the Lord, because of the wise counseling of my friend, I turned to Him."

Well, good for you. Throw you a Bozo button. I'm so glad you had it all together and I didn't. Well, mister, there's one major difference between your story and mine. You said it yourself that some inexperienced driver killed your family. Well, it was my prayers that killed my parents.

No longer able to stand the battle raging inside her, Olivia leapt out of her seat and bolted out the door. Tears blurred her vision as she ran outside and into the woods behind the church. Erik and Audra called after her, but she pushed her legs faster and harder. Not caring where she ended up, she continued running until her lungs burned and she could no longer breathe. She hid behind a large oak tree and gulped in huge quantities of air, only stopping the breaths long enough for Erik and Audra to run past her. As they did, she slid around the gigantic tree trunk, opposite of them and then darted off.

Confident she had escaped, she found another large oak tree, removed her sweater, laid it on the ground, and sat on it. She buried her head in her hands and wept.

"There you are."

Olivia jerked her hands away from her face and slowly followed the long jean clad legs standing in front of her upward. Her eyes widened. "Hammond?"

"Oh, Livvy." A twig snapped as Hammond knelt down and pulled her into his arms.

This couldn't be happening. Hammond was—was dead.

Olivia stiffened. She refused to be comforted by the man who had let her believe he was dead all this time. Yanking courage to herself, she shoved him away and stood. "So it was you I saw at the airport. Why'd you run from me? What are you doing here? And where have you been?"

"No, Livvy. It's me, Haskell. Not Hammond."

Her forehead wrinkled. "What?" she blurted, shaking her head. Confusion yanked what remaining sanity she had from her. What was going on? She stared at the jacket she'd made for Hammond. "But… how did you…? You must be Hammond. That's his jacket. He was wearing it the day he got on that plane. I don't understand." Her head swayed back and forth, threatening to pitch her heart and soul onto the hard ground. She ran her fingers through her long curls. "I don't understand." Black spots danced before her eyes. The nightmare continued. In slow motion, she drifted to the ground, but she never felt herself hit the hard surface.

Chapter Fourteen

In slow motion, Olivia slumped toward the ground. Before she hit the dirt floor of the forest, a stout man scooped her up. Anger exploded in Erik so forcefully he thought he would blow a header. "Put her down! Now!" Erik barked the order. His insides vibrated with a mixture of anger and fear.

Olivia's eyes slowly rolled opened.

"I said put her down." Erik clenched his fists at his side, ready to use them if necessary. Olivia's bloodshot, sad, and desperate eyes ripped at his heart. He wanted to hold her in his arms and will all of her pain into himself.

"Haskell." Her timid voice brought out the protective animal instinct inside of Erik. He took another step closer to the man she'd called Haskell.

Olivia squirmed in his arms. "Put me down." Her voice was weak and shaky.

The man slowly released her but never took his eyes off of Erik.

"What's going on here?" Erik looked at the stranger, then at Olivia.

She faced the man. "That's what I'd like to know." Olivia's tone sounded stronger this time.

"Livvy." Audra's breathless voice drew his attention that direction. Audra closed the distance between them.

Panting, she turned toward the man and asked, "Haskell? What are you doing here?"

"That's what I'd like to know." Disgust dripped from Olivia now. "And what are you doing with Hammond's jacket?"

Haskell ran his hand over his face. "Livvy. I'm sorry. I never meant to frighten you. I only wanted to see you. Can we go somewhere?" He glanced at Erik. "I'll explain it all then."

"No. Tell me now."

Yeah. Tell her now. Erik wanted to hear this too.

Olivia couldn't stop her insides or her knees from shaking. She picked up her sweater, laid it on a flat part of the large oak, and parked her backside onto the limb. Audra joined her, and Erik positioned his body sideways between Haskell and herself.

Haskell nodded and sighed. "Remember when I said I would explain to you someday why I was avoiding you?" He reached for her hand, but Olivia jerked it away.

His pained gaze went from Audra to Erik, then back to her. "Can we *please* talk in private?"

"No" She crossed her legs and straightened out her dress. "Quit stalling."

Again he looked at Erik, then back at Olivia. "I don't really know where to start. Until I knew for certain that Hammond was d—..." He closed his eyes and wet his lips. "I miss him something fierce." His chest rose and fell before he opened his eyes that were now filled with moisture. “I felt so guilty that I couldn’t face you.”

Olivia frowned. “You couldn’t face me? Why?”

“Well, the reason Hammond left that day wasn’t because he wanted to get to the hot air balloon races. It was because he was mad at me.”

“You? Why?”

“Because. We got into a big fight.” Tears slipped down his cheeks, and he squatted down in front of her. “Oh, Livvy. It’s all my fault. Hammond would still be alive if it hadn’t been for me.”

Olivia tried to process what he’d just said. What did he mean it was his fault? It was hers. Just like it was her fault that her parents were killed too.

“Remember right before Hammond left to go to the airport and we all went and had lunch together?”

Woodenly, Olivia nodded.

“I couldn’t believe Hammond openly flirted with that waitress. And right in front of you too.” His head slid from side to side. He stood and paced in front of the tree. “I was livid with him.”

Olivia looked up at Erik. The soft compassion in his eyes, that was surely meant to comfort her, only deepened her embarrassment. Erik pitied her. Well, she didn’t want his pity. She tore her attention from him and put it back onto Haskell.

“After we got to the airport and they warned Hammond not to fly because of the weather, you got mad at him and said if he wanted to kill himself to go ahead, but you weren’t going to stand around and watch. Remember?”

Boy did she. She remembered that moment as if it were yesterday. Fresh guilt tore at her heart.

"After you left, Hammond and I got into a big argument. I told him what a selfish pig he was for not taking into consideration how you felt. He asked me what I was talking about. I lit into him that he never even considered how hard his flying in bad weather was for you." Sympathy drifted through Haskell's eyes and into her.

"He admitted he hadn't even thought about that and had the decency to feel bad. But when I mentioned how hard it was for you to watch him openly flirt with other women, he laughed and said he was just having fun." Haskell snorted. "Yeah, fun at your expense."

He stopped pacing, looked at the ground, then back at her. "I told him it wasn't funny and that he was being a jerk. That he was blessed to have you. And that I'd give anything if I had someone like you for my fiancée. Hammond was no dummy. I tried to look away before he saw the truth in my eyes. But I wasn't fast enough. Hammond went ballistic. He accused me of being in love with you, of stabbing him in the back. He stormed out of the room and got into his plane and left." Haskell captured her gaze. "The truth is. Hammond was right. I was in love with you. I still am."

Olivia jumped to her feet. "You what?"

"I'm sorry. I couldn't help myself. Look at you. You're beautiful. You're intelligent, talented, and so sweet. When we met you that day at Blackwater Falls, I knew you were the one for me."

Whoa. This was too much for Olivia to absorb. She sat down again before she fell down from the shock of what she'd just heard.

"I told Hammond I was going to ask you out, but he said he'd beat me to it. Well, I loved him too much to go behind his back. But then, wasn't that what I was doing by secretly loving you, by wishing it was I who was with you, and not him?"

What exactly was one supposed to say to something like that? "I… I didn't know."

"Of course you didn't. No one knew. You see, Livvy." He gave a quick glance at Audra and Erik, then knelt down in front of her again and clasped her hands in his. "I'm responsible for Hammond's death. If I hadn't made him angry, he would have never gotten in the plane. And he would be alive today."

Even though Olivia's brain was on overload, she had to know one more thing. "How did you get his jacket?"

"He tossed it at me right before he stormed out the door. I held onto it, knowing how special it was to him because you had made it for him. I was going to give it to him when he got back. But then he never…" His Adam's apple rose and fell and a tear slid down his cheek. "I started wearing it so I would feel close to you and to him. That's why I'm here. I had to see you." He glanced nervously at Erik then back at her. "To be near you. The day you told me you were moving, I was so angry with you for leaving. First I lost Hammond, and then you. But then when I came to my senses, I realized you didn't even know I was in love with you."

Olivia pressed her fingertips against her forehead and shook her head. Shock, disbelief, relief and a million other emotions skittered through her soul. She wasn't responsible for Hammond's death? All this time, she thought she had made him so furious that he had to get as far away from her as possible.

One realization after another slammed into her. Perhaps she'd wronged God by blaming Him. Hammond did have a choice. In his anger, he'd made the wrong one. And that wrong choice had cost him his life. Just like Haskell felt guilty for Hammond's death, she felt guilty for her parents' death.

Like a bolt of lightning a new thought flashed through her mind, making her heart sink. Remorse flooded every inch of her being. Someone had told her a long time ago to be careful what you pray for. If only she would have known that the day her parents had left. Because that day, God had indeed answered her prayer.

"Livvy?" Erik reached out to her with only his voice and his gaze, but they were enough.

Olivia refused to let the tears backing up in her eyes flow. "Yes?"

"Are you okay?"

Olivia gave a nervous titter. There were those words again.

Haskell looked at her as if she'd lost her mind. And perhaps she had.

"No." She jerkily shook her head. "And I'll probably never be okay again." With those words she rose. "I wanna go now."

Everyone followed her, except Erik, who walked beside her. Again, he seemed to sense her need for silence because he said absolutely nothing. He just matched her stride for stride all the way out of the woods.

"Why did you run away from her at the airport?" Olivia heard Audra ask Haskell. "And how did you know where she was?"

"I've been following you." He had the good sense to sound guilty about it. "When you checked in your luggage, and I heard what flight you were taking, I checked to see if they had any more available seats. I only wanted to make sure she was happy; to make sure she was okay. When I saw her running from church, crying. I followed her."

"Well, I understand that, but don't you know you frightened her half to death standing outside her living room window?" Audra bit out.

"What are you talking about? I never stood outside her window."

Olivia stopped and spun toward Haskell. "Well, if it wasn't you, then who was it?"

That question haunted Erik all the way back to his pickup. He jogged over to Chase's truck and told them not to worry; he'd see them later on. Erik was grateful that they were going to help his aunt this afternoon because she needed it. And Olivia needed him.

It wasn't easy, but Erik stayed in the background as Olivia said her goodbyes to Haskell.

"You take care, Haskell."

Not a man normally given to jealousy, when Olivia and Haskell locked themselves in an embrace, Erik wanted to jerk the man's arms off of Olivia, but he restrained himself.

"You, too. I love you, Livvy."

Ache clawed at Erik's heart. The thought of someone else loving his Olivia unnerved him. Whoa. Since when had he started thinking of Olivia as his?

When Haskell left, Erik, Olivia, and Audra took their time as they headed toward Erik's truck. No one spoke, which Olivia deeply appreciated. So many questions squiggled through her brain, bombarding her frazzled emotions. A nap sounded great. She wanted to go home and bury herself under the blankets for days. But Olivia wouldn't do that to Adell. Instead, she forced herself to buck up and rise above her tumultuous situation. After all, she still had a busy day ahead of her.

Erik helped Olivia and Audra climb into his truck. Thick silence hung in the cab. He didn't have a clue what to say.

"Well, that was interesting," Audra piped up.

Simultaneously, in slow motion Erik and Olivia turned their heads toward the backseat.

Audra shrugged. "Anyone else as hungry as I am?"

She smiled cheekily.

Neither spoke. They faced forward, shaking their heads slightly. Olivia's friend sure was a unique bird.

"Okay, then. I'll take that as a yes," Audra chirped as if nothing was amiss. "We still going to Tamarack?"

Erik's gaze captured Olivia's. "I know it's been a stressful morning for you. Would you like to go home and get some rest before the party?"

He watched as she battled with what to do. "No." She shook her head. "Even if I went home, I don't think I'd be able to rest. I'd rather go ahead and go to Tamarack. I need something to take my mind off of everything that's just happened. And I've heard that place is great." Olivia looked toward the dash. "It's only 10:32. It takes a half an hour to get to Beckley. So that'll be just right. I'm sure my stomach will be growling by then." Her smile was forced.

"Thanks for the warning." Erik winked.

Everyone laughed, but Olivia's wasn't her normal cheery laughter. It, too, seemed forced.

On the way there, Audra regaled them with hilarious stories about women and their wild hair-dos, Louey her long haired Chihuahua's silly antics, and the kids' goofy larking about in children's church.

Glad the heavy fog inside the cab of his truck had lifted, Erik glanced over at Olivia. He thought about his growing feelings for her. One huge obstacle stood in the way of him telling Olivia how much he loved her. He didn't know where she was at with the Lord. Judging from her reaction in church, the answer to that question might pose more than just a little trouble for his heart. *Lord, I don't know what to do about this. Please, give Olivia Your peace and help her to find You.* He sighed. *She really needs You, Jesus.* And I really need her.

♥♥♥

Thirty minutes later, they pulled into the parking lot at Tamarack and started up the walk. The red roof with A-frame peaks reminded Olivia of a crown. Scanning the area, she noticed the yellow sculptured daffodils amongst the bright flowers and trees. Flowers, bushes, shrubs, trees, and lush greenery, including the walls of greenery lining the entrance were everywhere. The muted red and gray brick pathway inside the circle reminded Olivia of an old cobblestone street. Above the entrance, she read the sign, Caperton Center. To her left, a unique metal plaque with thirteen sculptured hands, said - Tamarack—The Best of West Virginia.

Inside, one look was all it took for Olivia to understand why the place was called, The Best of West Virginia. The very building itself spoke of class. Like the roof outside, the ceilings were lofty and peaked. Skylights gave the building an airy and open feeling. In front of her was a Tourist Information Center. On her left was a gourmet section that had wines, dry mixes, barbeque sauces, jellies, homemade syrups, honey, candies, and even pet treats. Just looking at all the food made Olivia's stomach growl.

"Hungry are we?" Erik asked from behind her.

Olivia tilted her head sideways and pursed her lips at

him. "What gave you the first clue?" Her smirk told him she was just teasing.

"I'm hungry too," Audra said from beside her, then looked at Erik. "Where's this Fried Green Tomato Sandwich you told us about? The one that Tamarack *is famous for*." Audra imitated Erik's earlier assessment of the place.

"Patience, Miss Audra. We'll go there in a few minutes." He looked at Olivia and smiled, then winked. Olivia ignored the way his wink made her stomach flip with giddiness.

Traveling down the circular walkway, at the Textile section Olivia stopped to admire the rugs, quilts, doilies, and aprons. At the Pottery section, Olivia was amazed at all the extraordinary pottery items in every shape and size imaginable, including bowls, cups, colanders, vases, and even mugs and jugs with caricature faces. Between the Glass and Wood sections was a Christmas Shop with fully decorated trees with handmade ornaments. Blown glass balls of all colors and shapes and sizes, crocheted angels, and snowflakes, filled the place. Like a fast moving locomotive, Olivia zipped through the Christmas shop. After her parents had died, she dreaded Christmas. It was just too depressing.

Across from Wood and Toys was a Metal department. Erik seemed particularly interested in that part of Tamarack. He soon became deeply engrossed in a quiet conversation with a gray-haired, female employee.

Giving him his privacy, they continued to look around until Erik finished.

This whole place was unlike anything she'd ever seen before. As an artist she appreciated all the love and long hours that went into creating such magnificent pieces such as the wooden carved trashcan with a mother bear holding the lid and her cubs climbing up the side. A unique barn wood trashcan sported a small chicken coop on top with a bed of straw and hens.

As they entered the food court, Olivia couldn't take it all in fast enough. More of West Virginia's finest hung on the walls and sat inside wooden cases on top of the wooden counters. Deli, Grill, and Bakery signs caught her eye. Her stomach growled again at the heavenly aromas wafting around them.

"C'mon. Let's eat before everyone thinks one of those carved bears came to life."

Eyes narrowed, Olivia slapped Erik's arm, then smiled.

Olivia debated between Tamarack's tuna melt, the trout with lemon brown butter, the chicken pot pie, or the fried green tomato sandwich.

"What's all in the Fried Green Tomato sandwich," Audra asked the waitress. "And what all does it come with?"

"Well," the blonde woman answered. "We dip the green tomatoes in batter, kind of like an onion ring batter. Then we put it on a bun with lettuce, tomato, bacon, and Swiss cheese. It comes with kettle style potato chips and dill pickle spear. Of course, you can add French fries if you wish, or Cole slaw."

They all looked at each other, smiled their approval,

and ordered the sandwich.

While eating their delicious sandwiches, Erik said, "This place has a dinner theater too."

Olivia's eyes widened. "Really?"

Erik locked gazes with her. "If you'd like, I can make theater reservations for us sometime."

Without giving a second thought to the ramifications of what his offer meant, Olivia nodded and popped the last bite of her sandwich in her mouth. As a slow eater, she was always the last one finished.

"Can we finish looking around now?" Audra asked.

"I'm ready." She looked at Erik. "How about you?"

"Yep."

Trash gathered, they threw it away in a nearby trashcan and finished making their way around Tamarack. The Art Gallery was Olivia's favorite. When they passed the Governor Hulett C. Smith Theater, Erik pointed it out to Olivia. Anticipation filled his eyes. The thought of spending time with Erik in a theater sent a thrill of excitement rushing through her, but with lightning quickness she brushed it aside.

Across the walkway from the theater, to the right, Erik made his way to a bronze and glass coffee table with a fisherman standing in a stream. Olivia wondered if he liked to fish. And what else he liked to do besides drive monster trucks. Right then, she realized how little she knew about the man she'd fallen in love with. Against her will. And against her better judgment. The man she would never allow herself to have. Shaking off the pit that had lodged in her heart, she focused her attention elsewhere and quickly started oohing an aahing over the variety of jewelry, wearable art, and scented candles.

When it was time to leave, Olivia had mixed emotions. She couldn't wait to go to his aunt's, but she hated leaving Tamarack and all of its artistic beauty.

"Why don't y'all go on?" Erik asked as they arrived near the exit. "I forgot something."

Audra stopped. "We could wait."

"No, no. That's okay. It'll only take a minute." He dug into his pocket, fished out his keys, and handed them to Olivia.

Outside, the afternoon sun warmed their air-conditioned skin.

They were so busy regaling about Tamarack that they didn't even notice Erik's arrival until they heard a click in the back bed of the pickup. Erik popped the toolbox open and then closed it.

"Ready, ladies?" he asked, hopping inside.

Thirty minutes later, they arrived back in Charity. Erik parked in front of a blond brick two-story house with a porch resembling a small antebellum plantation with white shutters on the windows. A three-foot wrought iron fence with matching brick pillars encased the front yard.

Erik shut off the truck, then helped Olivia and Audra out. They headed toward the front door. Decorative rock surrounded two flowering tulip trees. Bushes of West Virginia's state flower, rhododendron maximum, covered the yard. Olivia loved the big laurel's large dark evergreen leaves. Too bad they weren't blooming. The delicate pale pink and white blooms, mottled with red and yellow flecks were gorgeous.

When they stepped onto the last of the three wooden steps, the front door swung open. "Hello, hello." Adell, dressed in pastel yellow, stood on her tiptoes and gave Erik a big hug. Then she turned to Olivia. "It's so nice to see you again." She gave Olivia a long squeeze. "Welcome to my home."

"Thank you for having me." Olivia turned toward Audra. "Mrs.—"

His aunt held up a finger. "Adell, remember." Her eyes smiled like Erik's.

Olivia nodded. "Adell, this is my dear friend, Audra Darron. Audra, this is Erik's aunt, Adell."

"Pleased to meet you, ma'am." Audra extended her hand, but Adell bypassed it and pulled her into a hug.

Erik's aunt seemed to hug anyone within arm's reach. All doubts about bringing a guest vanished. Olivia bet this woman didn't know a stranger.

"Well, come on in." Adell stepped back and motioned for them to enter. Inside, Olivia marveled at the Civil War antiques that filled the room. But the thing that caught her attention the most was the life-sized portrait near the fireplace. She stopped to admire it. The woman in the picture was a younger version of Adell. And the girl, sitting in front of the woman and the handsome, dark haired, mustached gentleman looked just like him.

"God sure did bless me with a handsome husband and beautiful daughter. God rest their souls."

Olivia swung her gaze toward Adell who had strolled up next to her. What did she mean God rest their souls?

Erik stepped up behind her. His presence made breathing and thinking difficult for her. "My uncle passed away about twenty years ago. And their only daughter died of leukemia when she was ten."

The words spiked through Olivia's brain. She couldn't believe it. Today, she'd learned that two other families had lost loved ones too. And yet, neither one of them seemed to be angry with God, nor had they turned their backs on Him. The pastor's words floated through her mind. *Sometimes guilt causes us to turn away from God, instead of to Him.*

"Well, come along." Adell turned toward the back of the house, acting as if nothing was amiss.

Didn't Adell miss them? Wasn't she bitter?

The three of them followed their hostess through the house. Cinnamon, spice, smoked barbeque and other delicious smells permeated everything. Olivia's stomach rumbled.

Adell stopped and tilted her head. "What was that?"

Olivia sent both Erik and Audra a warning glare.

"Nothing, Aunt Adell," Erik said, barely containing his smile. "Nothing."

When they stepped out onto the covered patio, Olivia gasped. People covered nearly every square-inch of the huge back yard. A line of every colored rose imaginable lined the immaculate yard that stopped within mere feet of a pond loaded with blooming lily pads. Two trees stood like guards at the end of yard. On each side of them, about ten feet away, were the biggest marble planters Olivia had ever seen. Each overflowed with trailing greenery and a variety of bright flowers.

On her right, in the corner near the patio was a good eight-foot cherub water fountain. Mouth agape, Olivia stared at the three large canopy covers with long tables decorated with several purple centerpieces. Did Adell know that purple was her favorite color, or was it just a coincidence? Somehow, Olivia didn't think it was. Never in her whole life had she seen anything or any place more beautiful. This place was the epitome of Adell. Beautiful inside and out.

"Hey," Camara greeted them as she breezed by them carrying two full pitchers of what looked to be sweetened tea. "I'll catch up with y'all later," she hollered over her shoulder.

Before Olivia could respond, a short chubby lady grabbed her hand and shook it until Olivia thought it might pull from its socket. "Hello. You must be Olivia."

"Olivia, this is my neighbor, Ethel Briggs," Adell said from beside her.

Name after name passed through Olivia's brain. No way would she ever remember them all. Erik stayed close to her side the whole time. Miss Bubbly-Outgoing Audra, however, mingled with all the guests, making ado over this and that.

Later on in the evening, Olivia tried desperately to focus on the wonderful party thrown in her honor, but she just couldn't shake the portrait image from her mind. She had to go back in and see it. "Erik."

"Yeah?" He turned those soft brown eyes on her.

"Where's the restroom?" Heat filled her cheeks.

"I'll show you."

"No, no. Don't be silly. Just tell me. I can find it."

Erik studied her face for a moment, then explained where it was.

After refreshing herself, she made her circuitous way back through the large house and into the room with the portrait. Hands behind her back, she stopped in front of the painting and focused her attention on it. A connection to the young girl in the picture spiked through her spirit. What pain she must have suffered from the leukemia. Olivia could relate. Not to the leukemia, but to the young girl's pain.

Tears slipped over her eyelashes and onto her cheek. With one swipe, she brushed them away, and looked around, making sure she was alone. Olivia knew she should get back to the party, but she just wasn't ready to yet. She stared up at the blue-eyed girl. The poor thing died when she was only ten. The same age as Olivia when her parents had died.

Frustration invaded her soul. As long as Olivia lived, she would never understand why exceptionally cruel people like her aunt Hattie lived long lives, and young, sweet innocent, good-hearted people, like the young girl in the portrait and her parents, died premature deaths. Even more befuddling to her, was that those who were left behind were expected to go on living as if nothing happened. At least that's what Olivia had been taught anyway.

Right after her parents' death, when grief overtook Olivia, and her aunt discovered her crying, the wicked woman would backhand her across the face and snarl, "You're parents are gone. Dead. Caput. They ain't never comin' back. So, jist git over it." Each time Olivia heard the word dead, she sobbed harder. And each time her aunt bit out, "You want somethin' ta cry about, gurl. Then, I'll give you somethin' ta cry about." Even now Olivia felt the cruel yank on her hair, the jerking of her arm, and the slamming of her body against the wall.

But the bone-crunching pain of hitting the wall had never compared to the excruciating pain of her loss. Moisture slid down over her cheeks. "Oh, Mom, Dad, I miss you so much. And, Mom. I didn't mean what I said. Honest. I'm so sorry God answered my prayers to never see you again." Her shoulders shook. "My prayers killed y'all. I'm so sorry." Her chin dropped to her chest as tears flooded her eyes.

"Oh, Honey."

Olivia whirled toward the gentle voice. Mortified, she quickly swiped at her eyes and wiped the moisture on her dress.

Adell stood there at the threshold to the room. Slowly the older woman walked toward her. "I didn't mean to eavesdrop, sweetie, but God didn't answer that prayer. He would never kill your parents." The compassion in Adell's eyes caused rivers of tears to gush from Olivia's.

"I'm sorry," Olivia said between sobs. "I didn't know anyone was around."

"C'mon." Adell extended her wrinkled hand. "We need to talk. Let's go to my bedroom."

"But," Olivia sucked in several ragged breaths. "Your party."

Her soft, understanding smile touched Olivia.

"They're playing games and havin' a ball. They won't even know we're gone. And Erik thinks I've come in here to check on you."

Seeing no other way out and really wanting to hear what Adell had to say, Olivia let herself be led to a back bedroom where they sat down on a handmade quilt spread across a four-poster bed. Adell reached across and snatched a box of tissues off the nightstand. She yanked a couple out and handed them to Olivia. She wiped her eyes and blew her nose with one.

"Now, tell me why you think God answered your prayers and killed your parents."

Olivia couldn't believe how comfortable she felt around this woman. The kindness in her eyes, and the compassion in her voice, along with the weariness of carrying this heavy burden for so long, gave Olivia the courage she needed to spill her heart out.

"The day my mom and dad were to go on a missionary trip was the day before my tenth birthday." Olivia twisted the tissue in her hand. "I was so angry with them because they were going to miss my birthday again. Three years in a row, they were gone on my birthday."

She sucked in a long shaky breath. "Nothing I said or did persuaded them not to go. When we got to the airport, I tried one more time. I begged them not to leave. I told them they loved God more than me. Mom tried to assure me that that wasn't true. She said Daddy and her were called by God to take His message into the world and that they were sorry that their scheduled times always seemed to land on my birthday."

She looked at Adell. "Mom thought by giving me lots of presents and by having Mimi arrange a party for me that everything would be okay. Well, it wasn't. I wanted my parents there." Her gaze fell to her lap. "I know it was selfish, but it just wasn't the same without them. It seemed like every important event in my life, my parents had to fly off to some foreign country for God." She blankly stared at the mangled tissue in her hand. "I started to not care for God at all. After all, He was constantly taking my parents away from me.

"The day they died." She paused, sniffing. Tucking her lower lip between her teeth to keep it from trembling, she strove to gain even the smallest measure of composure. Her chest heaved a few times before she continued, "By the time we got to the airport, I was so angry. When they hugged me and promised me that we would do something special together as a family when they got back from doing the Lord's work, I lost it. I jerked away from them." She sniffed, and Adell pressed another tissue in her hand. "I yelled that I couldn't care less if we ever did anything together again."

Streams of tears rushed from Olivia's eyes. "I told them I hated them, and then I prayed God would just keep them wherever they were going because I never wanted to see them again." Olivia dropped her face into her hands. Her whole body shook with uncontrollable sobs.

Adell wrapped Olivia in her arms and lovingly pressed her head against her shoulder. "There, there, sweetie." Adell rocked her and gently removed the strands of hair that clung to Olivia's tear-soaked face.

"It's all my fault they're dead. I should have never said that," she whimpered. "And it's my fault that Mimi died and that Hammond died too. God's punishing me for being so selfish."

"Ah, sweetie. That's not true. First of all, God doesn't punish us. He disciplines us sometimes, but He doesn't punish us. And He certainly doesn't go around killing people because a ten-year-old girl was hurt and said some things she didn't mean. If that was the case, we'd all be dead. Because at one time or another all of us have wished someone would just die and never come back. I know I sure did." The older woman's chest expanded. "For a long time, I felt exactly like you do. The day my husband died, I had said something similar to him."

Olivia pulled out of her arms and searched the older woman's eyes, looking to see if she was being honest. Adell never blinked or removed her gaze from Olivia's. "My Henry was a train engineer. He loved it more than anything else in this life. At least that's what I thought."

Olivia could relate. She thought her parents loved missionary work more than her.

"Anytime someone called in sick, or they needed a replacement, Henry would go. I constantly begged him not to go, to stay home and spend time with me and Sarah. The day he died, I, too, yelled at him. I told him to just pack his bags and to not bother coming home. I was tired of competing with a locomotive. When the policeman came to my door and told me my Henry was gone, that he'd been crushed between two railroad cars, I felt the full weight of those words, and I've never been sorrier for any words I've ever spoken."

Olivia's hand flew to her mouth. "How awful."

"It was. And I beat myself up for years over it. I felt like it was my fault that he died. I felt so guilty that I couldn't even pray or anything. Then two years later Sarah died. I was so mad at God that I didn't go to church or pray or anything for a long time. I basically hid from the world."

"You were angry at God, too?" Olivia couldn't keep the shock from her voice or face.

"Yes, I was. Until Erik's mom, my sister, came out to see me. Just being around her sweet gentle spirit, reminded me of how much I missed God. I knew I had to make a choice. To either remain angry at God and to continue blaming Him for not healing my daughter or keeping Henry safe, or to give my grief and guilt over to Him."

This morning the pastor had said almost the same thing. Slowly Olivia's mind stopped spinning, and the confusion finally began to settle. "When my parents died in that plane crash, I blamed God. I loathed Him for taking them from me. But the real reason I didn't want anything to do with Him anymore was because of my own guilt. I truly believed my prayer is what killed them." Olivia turned her body, facing Erik's aunt. "What did you do? You know. To get God to forgive you."

"I asked."

Olivia's jaw slackened. "That's it?"

"Yes. Sis told me that God had never left me, that it was me who had left Him."

This surprised Olivia. She thought for certain it was God who had abandoned her. After all, she didn't want

Him to love her anymore, especially when she heard that He punishes those He loves.

"Sis said to pour my heart out to Him and to cast the care of my burdens, guilt, and shame onto Him. I even had to ask God to help me to love Him again because I certainly didn't feel it at the time. I realized I'd really missed Him, but I didn't love Him. Or so I thought. But what I found was that feelings have very little to do with my relationship with Christ. Faith does, but feelings don't. Feelings are too fickle. Mine certainly were.

"Let me tell you, Olivia, once I gave it over to God, it took time and work to get my relationship back to where it once was. But, I'm so glad I did." Adell's eyes lit up. Her whole countenance glowed and love emanated from her. Olivia felt the warmth of that love. A love that seemed vaguely familiar to her. But where and when? Then it hit her. It was the same kind of love she felt as a child, standing in church, with her arms raised, worshipping God. During that time, His loving presence filled the church. It was almost tangible.

At that moment, Olivia realized she missed God too. She wanted—no needed—His forgiveness. His comfort. His healing. But most of all, she needed His love.

"Adell." Olivia lowered her eyelids, then captured Adell's gaze. "Would you p—pray with me?"

"I'd love to, honey."

They bowed their heads. Right there, Olivia poured her heart out to the Lord. She confessed her anger toward Him. She asked for, and even felt the receiving of His forgiveness.

"And, Lord," Adell added when Olivia was done, "cleanse Olivia and heal her heart and mind from all the pain of the past. Thank you, Lord, that You took what the devil meant for Olivia's destruction, and You turned it around for good."

Olivia's eyes darted open, and she jerked her head toward Adell, who seemed completely oblivious to what she'd just said. That was the third time Olivia had heard those words. Maybe, just maybe, God hadn't forgotten her after all.

"Amen." Erik whispered from outside his aunt's bedroom door. He backed away and wiped the tears from his eyes. Now, he finally understood why God had moved him to West Virginia. Olivia would have never met his aunt. And she might never have poured her heart out to someone who completely understood how she felt. But when God's timing was right, He knew just the person Olivia could talk to. Someone who understood her pain and could help her.

Unfathomable joy welled up inside him. Not only did Olivia rededicate her life to the Lord, but now he could pursue a relationship with her. "Praise You, Lord," he whispered through tears. "Thank You so much."

Not wanting Olivia to know he had eavesdropped on their conversation, he slipped back down the hallway and went outside. The courting candle he'd bought at Tamarack would come in pretty handy now.

Chapter Fifteen

Olivia opened her eyes and glanced at the clock. 11:37. As she stretched, memories of the previous day cascaded on her, but for the first time in forever, they were peaceful memories, good memories. She smiled. "Lord, today is the first day of the rest of my life. I want to start off by talking to You. I've spent too many years away. I don't ever want to do that again."

Audra tapped on her door.

"Come in."

Her friend opened the door and peeked around. "I thought I heard you talking to someone."

"I was."

Audra glanced around the room. "Uh, did I just enter fantasy land here?"

Olivia fluffed her pillows then rested them against the flower-shaped headboard. She sat up, and pressed her back into the downy softness and patted the bed. Audra trotted in and leapt up onto it. Crossing her legs Indian style, she stared at Olivia as if she'd lost her mind.

"I was talking to God."

Audra's chin dropped. Her eyes bulged. For several seconds she sat like that.

"You're catching flies, Audie."

Audra snapped her lips back into place. "What do you

mean you were talking to God?"

"Oh, Audie." She tossed the covers off and edged closer to her best friend. "I would have told you last night, but it was so late, and I was so tired. And, well, all I wanted to do was bask in what happened." Olivia replayed the scene from the night before for Audra.

"Oh, Livvy. I'm so happy." They tossed their arms around each other and hugged. "My prayers have been answered."

They pulled back, and Olivia smiled at her friend. "Thanks, Audie for praying for me, and for never giving up on me. I know I bit your head off every time you told me that you loved me and so did Jesus. But, I just couldn't stand to hear it. I hope you understand that."

"Of course I do. I love you, Livvy."

"I love you too."

"And so does Jesus." Audra's lips bowed into a smirk.

"He sure does." Olivia's smile was filled with deep appreciation.

Audra straightened. "More than you know, dear heart." Her eyes brightened. "God loves you so much that He orchestrated this whole thing."

"What whole thing?"

"Well, first of all, He moved you here to Charity, and gave you a fabulous job working for a very Godly man. He provided you with this beautiful home, and surrounded you with kind and generous neighbors. He even set up us going to church yesterday." She slowly shook her head. "And not just any church, but a church where the pastor has gone through something similar to you. Then," her voice escalated with excitement. "The one day you go there, the Holy Spirit has him teach on grief and turning your back on God."

Olivia's eyes widened. "The Holy Spirit did that?"

"Yes. Yes, He did. Why do you ask?" Audra slanted her head.

"Because yesterday, when I was sitting in church and that pastor was talking, he was saying everything I was thinking and things that only you and your parents knew. A few of the things Erik knew too. I kept wondering who'd told that pastor about my life. I even thought you had somehow talked to that worship leader and that pastor. That you and Erik had somehow set me up."

"Hey, I'm good. But I'm not *that* good." Audra's teasing tone brought a smile to Olivia's face. "But wait. It gets even better. God laid it on Adell's heart to throw you a party. And well, you know what happened there." Audra's face simply glowed.

Touched beyond measure, Olivia whispered. "I hadn't thought about that." It was mind boggling and very humbling to think that the God of the universe, the One that sent Jesus to die for mankind's sin, loved her that much. In fact, He loved her so much that He took the trouble of orchestrating every little detail for someone who had turned their back on Him. She sniffed and raised her face toward heaven. "Thank You so much, Lord."

"Yes, Lord. Thank You," Audra added.

Sniffing, they hugged each other and then sat in silence for a couple of minutes.

Revived and refreshed, and feeling better than she had

in years, Olivia looked at her best friend. "Let's do something fun today. I have the day off. Ya wanna go for a swim or something?"

"How come you don't have to work today?"

"Erik said I'd had enough excitement for one day, and that I needed a break. So, he gave me the day off."

The phone rang. Olivia snatched up the receiver on the nightstand and clicked Talk. "Hello." Silence. "Hello?" She could tell someone was there, but they didn't say anything. She pulled the phone away from her ear and clicked End. "Wrong number."

The same thing happened three more times. The fifth time Olivia smashed the Talk button and growled out, "Listen, if you want to talk, then talk. If not, don't call here again."

"Olivia?"

"Erik?"

"Yeah."

"Have you been trying to call me?"

"No. Why?"

"Um. Never mind. What can I do for you?"

"I wanted to see if it was okay if I brought lunch out to you and Audra. Aunt Adell sent all those leftovers home with me, and I didn't want them to go to waste."

"More leftovers, huh?" She snickered. "Just a minute. I'll ask Audra if she minds." She covered the mouthpiece with her hand and asked Audra if she cared. Which she didn't.

"Sounds good to us."

"Great. I'll have Mickie heat them up. I'll be there in

about twenty-five minutes."

"Sounds good." She hung up. Two seconds later the phone rang again.

She laughed as she pressed the Talk button. "Did you forget something?"

"Yeah. I forgot to @*~%# you."

Olivia's heart tilted at the vile words. She dropped the phone.

"What's wrong?" Audra snatched up the receiver. "Hello? Who is this?"

Olivia stared at the phone as if it were a stinging scorpion.

"What do you mean it's none of my business? What do you want?" Anger singed Audra's voice. Her eyes narrowed. "Creep. Don't ever call here again." She jerked the phone away from her ear and jammed the End button.

"What'd he say?" Olivia rubbed her fingers and thumbs rapidly.

"Nothing worth repeating. We'd better call the police." Audra pressed the Talk button.

"No wait!" Olivia jerked the phone away from Audra and shut it off. "There's something vaguely familiar in the tone of his voice." It almost reminded her of Ben's.

"So? Who cares? Look, some guy is harassing you. It needs to stop. I'm calling the police."

"I wouldn't do that iffen I were you, darlin'."

Olivia and Audra screamed and whirled toward the voice. A medium built man wearing a black ski masked stepped inside her bedroom.

"You should really learn ta lock yore door 'fore goin'

ta bed at night, darlin'."

Her brain scrambled. She did lock the door. Olivia chanced a glance at Audra, who paled. She must have gone outside this morning.

The man pulled a cord out of his pocket.

Fear rushed into Olivia's heart, making it pump triple time.

The intruder stepped closer to Olivia and handed her the rope. "Tie yore friend up. And you'd better make shore it's nice an' tight. Or I'll make it worse on ya, darlin'."

That voice. Olivia had heard it somewhere before. But where? Someone else used to call her darlin'. But who? "Who are you? What do you want?"

"I already told ya on the phone, darlin'." He closed the distance between them. Grabbing her wrist, he jerked her to him. "I'm hurt that ya forgot me already."

Olivia frowned. That tone. That pitch. The words themselves. So familiar and yet…

"Don't ya remember me tellin' ya that I'd get even with ya someday? Well, I'm here ta make good on that promise."

"Markus?" she squeaked. Her knees almost gave out, but she locked them into place.

He removed his mask and shoved it in his pocket. "In the flesh." Pure evil slashed through his eyes, making her queasy.

Images of him forcing himself on her, ripping at her blouse, and yanking on the zipper of her pants flashed through her mind. When he'd said he'd get even with her, she thought he meant by sabotaging her from getting employment. Not… She never dreamt that he meant… She sucked in her bottom lip.

He yanked open her hand and laid the rope there. "Do it."

Jesus, I know I haven't come to You in a long time, and I'm not even sure how to pray. But would You please keep Audra and I safe? She gulped as she looked into Audra's horror-stricken face.

"Don't worry, darlin'. I saved a piece of rope jist fer you." He glanced at her bed then back at her. That same lustful look he had that day at work was there again. Only there was no co-worker to rescue her this time. "It won't be that bad, darlin'. I promise."

Her stomach lurched. *Oh, God, have mercy on me. Please, help me.*

Stall. The word was more like a command than a suggestion. "How did you find me?" She fidgeted with the cord.

"Simple. I knew Audra would lead me to ya. I kin be a very determined man when there's something I want. Ya shoulda remembered that."

Olivia glanced at Audra. Apology and remorse covered her face and eyes. Olivia sent her a silent signal it was okay. How would she know that Markus would follow her? But now it all made sense. "So it was you standing outside my living room window."

"Sure was, darlin'. Now quit stallin'. I came to git even, and git even, I will."

♥♥♥

Erik drove down the driveway. Just off the road, the sun glinted on something shiny. He glanced over toward the base of the trees where he spotted the white Jeep, facing the two-track trail through the forest. His mind scrambled to remember what Olivia had said. She asked if he had just called. He'd had a sinking feeling when she'd said that. After all, it wasn't Haskell outside Olivia's window that night. Or so he'd said.

Erik slammed on his brakes. He didn't know if he was just being paranoid or not, but he didn't want to take any chances. He shut off his truck, reached inside his glove box, and grabbed the revolver he kept there. Property rights and the Second Amendment still meant something in West Virginia. After checking it for bullets, he opened his door and cautiously made his way toward Olivia's house.

He was twenty-yards away when he heard screams. Clutching the gun, he ran toward the porch. At the door, he quietly wiggled the handle. Locked. He heard voices coming from the direction of Olivia's bedroom. Erik snatched the spare house key from under a rock. Then as fast as he could, he ran around back. Pressing his body against the house, he proceeded toward the French doors of her bedroom. The blinds were drawn with the exception of a one-inch gap. Through the crack, he saw a man on the other side of the room, his back to the doors, holding a gun at Audra and Olivia.

Erik's adrenaline kicked into high gear. *Lord, please show me what to do. And whatever happens please keep Olivia and Audra safe.*

Courage and determination settled in him.

The man stepped near Olivia, turned her toward Audra, then waved the gun at her. They were only five feet away from Erik.

Heart pounding, he laid his hand on the French door and carefully tested the knob. Locked. With great care he inserted the key and turned it.

It clicked.

Erik held his breath.

Peering through the slat, he heaved a sigh of relief. The man hadn't flinched. He was focused solely on the two women.

Erik patiently waited to make his move. It would come. Of that he was perfectly sure.

Movement by the door snagged Erik's attention. Samson crept into the room.

The motion caught the man's attention, and he turned sideways, his aim away from the ladies.

Erik burst into the room.

The man whirled.

A gun fired.

Erik tackled the man to the ground, jerked his weapon from his hand, and tossed it out of the way.

Rough hands clutched Erik's neck, making him wheeze.

Supernatural strength possessed Erik. He jerked the man's hands off of him with a single yank. Three consecutive blows to the intruder's face, and he fell unconscious.

Erik yanked his gaze toward the frightened women.

"Hand me that rope, Olivia. Call the police, Audra." Erik barked orders, and they followed without question.

He tied the man up, making sure the knots were good and tight before he stood.

"Oh, Erik." Olivia ran into his open arms and clutched him. "Praise God you didn't get shot." She spoke into his neck, her warm breath evoking a shiver. He held her trembling body close to his. Their pounding hearts beat as one.

"I don't know what I would do if someone else I loved died." She gasped. "Lands o' Goshen." Olivia jolted back.

Erik pulled her back into his embrace, terrified that he almost lost her. He wanted to meld her against him and never let go. He peered over at the unconscious man and cringed at how close he'd come to tragedy. Thank God he'd listened to the Lord's prompting.

"I… I didn't mean that I love, love you. What I meant was..."

Erik leaned back. Her pink cheeks and gorgeous turquoise eyes tattled on her. She did too love him. His already racing heart ramped up a few more rpms. Only the increase in his heart rate had nothing to do with the adrenaline surge from a few minutes ago, but the excitement of knowing that his Olivia loved him. "Livvy. It's okay if you love, love me." He snagged her gaze. While his body was still trying to idle down from what had transpired, he breathlessly said, "Because I love, love you too."

Her eyes went wide. "You…you do?"

"Yes. I have for a long time." His attention touched on

her mouth.

"You…you have?" She licked her lips. He could still see the fear in her eyes. He longed to kiss it away, to let her know she was safe with him. Rather than resisting the urge, he nodded, slowly dipping his head until their lips met in a sweet, lingering kiss. Erik's body trembled under her touch. The woman could sure kiss.

"Well, it's about time, you two."

Erik jerked his head up. Both of them turned toward Audra.

"Praise the Lord. My prayers have been answered." Audra's hands and face were raised toward heaven.

Turning his tender gaze to Olivia, their eyes locked. "Mine too," he lovingly whispered. "Mine too."

Chapter Sixteen

Sunday morning, Olivia awoke with a huge smile. The night before she'd dreamt of her wedding day. One filled with thousands of lights, candles, and flowers everywhere. The sweetness of it stayed with her even after she and Erik had dropped Audra off at the Beckley airport and headed toward Ansted in Fayette County for their first official date.

"You ready for an adventure?" Erik asked, putting his arm around her shoulders and pulling her closer as he made his way toward Hawks Nest State Park.

Was she? She turned her head toward Erik. Seeing the childlike excitement in his face, she snuggled her head onto his shoulder. "I am." And she meant it. Olivia still couldn't believe she was doing two things she said she'd never do again. Falling in love and going on an adventure. It had to be God. There was no other explanation for it.

Erik pulled up to an unusual looking place, parked the truck, and shut it off. Olivia read: See The Unbelievable—Mystery Hole.

She turned toward Erik. "This is your idea of an adventure?"

"Just wait. You'll see." Erik paid for their tour, and they walked outside and around the corner to the entrance.

Once inside, Olivia clutched Erik's arm and stopped

him. "Oh no. I'm not allowed to go in there."

He turned puzzled eyes at her. "Why not?"

"Because. See that sign?"

Erik looked at it then back at her. "Yeah. So?"

"There's a part in that warning that pertains to me." She pointed to it and heaved a heavy sigh. "'People with heart ailments' Well," She pursed her lips and shook her head. "That's me. I have a heart ailment."

Concern clouded his eyes. "Really? You didn't tell me that. What heart ailment?" He grabbed her hands and searched her face.

Olivia couldn't keep the mirth from her eyes or lips. "My heart ails with love for you, Erik."

His body relaxed, and a smile lit up his whole face. "Well, in that case I'd better not go in there either because we seem to be suffering with the same ailment." He pulled her into his arms. When their lips touched, her heart danced, and love spread through her body.

"U-hm. Excuse me."

Olivia broke the kiss and looked over at a young man who had a silly grin on his face.

"Oh, sorry." She blushed.

They moved out of his way and let him pass. Arms wrapped around each other's waist, they entered The Mystery Hole.

No wonder they declared this place to be a gravity-defying wonder. Everything inside gave the illusion of doing just that—a ball rolling up hill, a tour guide sitting on the walls, and much more. By the time they got through it, Olivia had to hold onto Erik to stay standing, and something about the way he held her made her think he didn't mind that much.

After the tour was over, they got in his truck and drove to a little roadside stop east of Gauley Bridge. They sat under a covered picnic table and ate their creamy biscuits, sliced ham and southern fried apples that Mickie had packed. When they finished, they followed the trail. Olivia sucked in her breath at the spectacular view. Arms wrapped round each other, standing in silence, they stared at the incredible scene before them. Precipitous-sided cliffs of stone encapsulated the falls. The waters tumbled in a continual succession of falls and glittery spillovers. God had outdone himself on this one.

"Would you like to go see Hawks Nest Dam?" Erik asked, gazing down at her.

"No." Olivia's head vacillated. "I've heard the water can rise pretty rapidly there." She wanted an adventure, but not quite that big of one. "Could we just stay here a little longer?"

"Sure." Love flowed from his eyes to hers as he hugged her closer.

The falls were beautiful, the day perfect. But even perfection must come to an end. And so, an hour and half later, they pulled in front of Olivia's house. "I had a wonderful time, Erik." Awe filled her voice.

"Me, too." He paused. "Hey, how about next Friday we go to see a movie?"

"Sounds great."

Erik unlatched their seat belts and pulled her into his arms. He lowered his head and melded his parted lips with hers. Every part of her danced with joy as Erik continued to pour his love into her through his kiss. Moments later, breath mingling, he whispered, "I love you, Livvy."

"I love you, too," her heart answered for her.

He opened the truck door and helped her down. Hand-in-hand, they walked to her front door where he wrapped her in his arms and kissed her briefly. "Goodnight, sweetheart."

"Goodnight."

Then, without warning, he crushed her to him and took full possession of her mouth.

Her arms slipped around his neck. She matched each move he made and then some. With her heart backing her lips, she allowed them to fully reveal all the love she felt for him.

Minutes passed. Erik raised his mouth and in a breathless whisper said, "I need to go."

His masculine voice sounded slightly broken and softer than normal. Chills raced up and down Olivia's spine. He backed up and gave her a tremulous smile.

Olivia only nodded. She couldn't speak. Her lips tingled, and her heartbeat pulsated in her ears. So this was what true love felt like? The second her mind released that thought, fear attacked her, leaving her without a single breath.

Erik unlocked her door, flipped the light switch on, and stepped back. Olivia stepped inside. Still shaken, she masked her feelings, and gave him a peck on the cheek. She shut the door and leaned against it. "Lord, I need Your help here. I'm so scared, Father. I love Erik so much, but

I'm still not over my fear of losing yet another loved one."

As she stood there, her back against the door, she spotted her Bible on the living room end table. She shoved herself away from the door and skittered to it. Lowering herself onto the couch, she let her Bible fall open. Deuteronomy 30:19 snagged her gaze. *I call heaven and earth as witnesses today against you, that I have set before you life and death, blessing and cursing; therefore choose life, that both you and your descendants may live.*

As surely as she was sitting there, Olivia knew then that the choice was up to her. No one else could make it for her. She'd endured enough hardship in her life. And she'd allowed that hardship to keep her from living. Well, no more. From this moment on, she'd choose life. And if that life included Erik, she'd definitely take it.

God's peace surged through her spirit, soul, and body. Olivia saw a vision of the cascading water at Cathedral Falls. The walls encapsulating the majestic sight reminded Olivia of the stone walls she'd erected around her heart. That day at Adell's, when she'd repented of having an evil heart of unbelief in departing from the living God, a huge boulder had broken loose from her. Each sin she'd confessed: anger, rejection, bitterness, self-loathing, condemnation, guilt, one by one, they chipped away at her self-erected wall. The only obstacle left was fear.

Olivia bowed her head, "Father, forgive me for allowing fear to rule my life. Your Word says that, *You have not given us a spirit of fear, but of power, and of love, and of a sound mind.* You also said, *There is no fear in love; but perfect love casts out fear, because fear involves torment. But he who fears has not been made perfect in love.* Lord, I've lived in fear long enough. I've been tormented long enough. Perfect me in your love, Jesus. Break the stronghold of fear off of my life. Give me a sound mind in Jesus' name. Amen."

Joy unlike any she'd ever known before flooded her. Now ready to live her life, Erik's face uploaded into her memory banks. Of their own accord, the corners of her lips arched upward. Only God knew what the future held. Whatever it was, she knew she could trust God to handle it.

♥♥♥

Months of dating, working together, and getting to know each other had been better than Erik could ever have imagined. He'd finally decided that today was the day he would give Olivia the gift he'd gotten her at Tamarack. He loved her and wanted to be with her more each day. In fact, each time it was getting harder and harder to drop her off at the door.

He pulled his pickup in front of her house, grabbed the box from the seat, headed to her door, and knocked.

In seconds, Olivia opened the door. "Hi!" Her eyes lit up. The turquoise blouse she had on brought out the incredible color in her eyes. The turquoise and black belt looping through her black pants, hugged her small waist, and the pants hung loosely over her hips and thighs. Hair pinned back on the sides, the rest of her long, liquid-caramel tresses flowed freely down her back.

"Hi, sweetheart." Erik leaned over and kissed her

tenderly.

She accepted his kiss then wrapped her fingers around his. "C'mon in."

They walked over to the sofa and sat down.

Nerves he hadn't expected attacked him. "I have something for you." Scarcely breathing, he handed her the wrapped gift.

Olivia tilted her head and looked at him quizzically. "It's not my birthday or anything."

"So?" He shrugged though his insides trembled. "Just open it."

Carefully she pulled at each tuck.

It was all Erik could do to control the urge to reach over and rip the paper off. "When you open it, I need to explain what it is."

She glanced up at him, gave a brief nod, then continued opening the package.

When she flipped the lid and removed the tissue paper, she pulled the object out. She sucked in her bottom lip and turned the object sideways, then she tipped it upside down and turned it back and forth. Finally she looked up him. "Uh, thanks." She frowned. "What is it?"

"It's a courting candle."

"A courting candle?" Both brows spiked.

"Olivia." Erik reached for her hand, willing his heart not to burst. "It's an early American custom. Kind of old fashioned, I know, but hear me out."

She nodded.

"When a young man went to court a young lady, the girl's father would light a candle. When the flame burned down to the candleholder, it was time for the young man to leave. How close to the spirals the father set the candle was dependent on how well he liked or disliked the young man." Erik demonstrated how to adjust the wooden pin. "Ollie, I want to court you."

"Ollie?" Confusion laced her voice. "Court me? Huh?"

Erik chuckled. "The day you came for an interview, I thought I was interviewing someone named Ollie. Only Ollie turned out to be you."

They laughed.

"With all my heart, I love you, Liv. I want the kind of courtship that leads to marriage. If you feel the same way about me, and you want to marry me eventually," Erik reached for the lighter inside the box, "then light this. The degree that you love me is the degree you'll adjust this." He showed her the wooden handle. "If it's up high, then that means you really love me. If you set it low, you don't. I'll have my answer then."

Nervous, Erik couldn't keep his knee from bouncing as he watched Olivia place her hands on the wooden peg. With precise and slow movements, she slid the peg all the way to the top of the curly-cued metal candleholder. Erik's heart skipped a beat. She placed the candle on top and lit it. Erik's heart ignited right along with the candle. "Does that mean you want to marry me someday?"

Olivia lowered her lids. Her cheeks turned pink. "No."

Erik's heart sank. "No. You don't want to marry me someday?" He couldn't keep the disappointment from his voice.

"Not someday." She captured his gaze and his hands.

"I've wasted too much time fearing love. If you want to court me, that's fine. But I'd just as soon forget the courting part and get right to the marrying part. And not just someday. But now."

Erik couldn't believe his ears. His heart soared. His Livvy loved him and had consented to marry him—before he'd even really asked. A thousand details attacked him then. No ring. No knee. And yet, as Erik set the courting candle on the end table, pulled Olivia into his arms, and kissed her soundly, he knew none of that truly mattered because she would one day be his. And soon he hoped. Against her soft lips, he asked, "Is tomorrow soon enough?"

Epilogue

Olivia still couldn't believe they'd put such a beautiful wedding together so quickly. In April, when they had decided to get married right away, Olivia knew nothing about planning a wedding. Adell and Erik's mom had offered to help and went right to work. Those two women were miraculous wedding planners. She and Erik wanted to be married in June. The month they'd met one short year ago.

In her hands was the most beautiful dress Olivia had ever seen. The second she'd shown interest in the Cinderella style gown, Mrs. Cole insisted on buying it for her. The woman was amazing. This evening, Olivia would have a mom again. That thought streamed-lined unfathomable joy through her. Could she get any happier than this? She didn't know how.

Olivia slipped into the wedding dress and pulled it up. "Audra, could you button me up, please?"

"Of course." While Audra worked on the tiny pearl buttons at the back, Olivia admired the breathtaking dress in the mirror. Her gown was nearly an exact replica of the one in her dream, but even better. She smiled. Again with the déjà vu. Only this time it was a fabulous déjà vu. Clear beaded crystals swept from her bodice past her waist, showing off her slim figure. The strapless dress sported a dropped waistline with a full, tulle ball skirt. Silk and white rose lace covered her bosom.

"There. All done." Audra took hold of her hand and spun her.

"Oh, Livvy." Audra squealed. "You look just like Cinderella."

She couldn't keep her mouth from turning upward and her white teeth from showing. "I feel like Cinderella"

Her friend grabbed her and hugged her. "I'm so happy for you. It's about time." She pulled away and looked Olivia straight in the eye. "I told you Jesus loved you."

"That you did." She nodded. "That you did. And to think I used to hate it. Well, not anymore. I love hearing it."

"I'm so glad. I was so worried about you."

"I know. Thanks for not bailing on me when things got tough and for sticking with me through it all, Audra."

"Hey, what are friends for?" Audra winked at Olivia. "Now it's my turn to have you help me." Audra walked over to the closet in Olivia's room and pulled out her maid of honor gown. "Hmm, I wonder why you chose blue instead of purple." She winked.

After her friend dressed, Olivia stood back, admiring her and the beautiful gown. The strapless chiffon gown, with a dropped waistline like her wedding dress, had a pale shade of blue around the bodice, and a web of medium blue beads that hugged Audra's waist and part of her hip. The pale blue skirt flowed to the floor.

"Okay, zip me up." Audra backed up to Olivia.

A knock sounded on the door. "It's time, Olivia."

Camara's voice came through loud and clear.

"Be there in a second."

Olivia snatched the headpiece Mrs. Cole had dropped off. The ring of greenery, mingled with white baby roses and tiny white lights shaped like a tiara, reminded her of a crown a princess would wear. "Battery operated lights are amazing, aren't they?"

Her friend smiled. "They sure are."

She turned for one last glance in the mirror, and her breath caught. Her long hair was pulled back on the sides. One curled strand dangled loosely in front of each ear. The rest flowed down her back, making her look and feel like a modern day Cinderella. And today she was marrying her very own Prince Charming.

Quickly, both she and Audra slid their feet into their silk flat shoes, picked up their flower bouquets, and headed toward the door.

"Wait! Stop!" Audra commanded.

Olivia froze. "What?"

Audra grabbed a tissue and held out her hand. "Give me the gum."

Olivia laughed and let the chewed up wad fall into the tissue.

"Oh, before I forget..." Audra snatched up her purse and pulled something out of it. "Erik told me to give you this." She placed the shiny new penny in Olivia's hand. "And he said to tell you that this penny isn't for your thoughts. It's to put in your shoe because your luck is about to change."

Touched beyond measure, Olivia sweetly tsked. "Ah-

h. That's so-o sweet. I could just cry."

"Not now." Audra sounded horrified. "You'll ruin your makeup."

Olivia released a nervous chuckle. She shook her head and smiled at her friend, who knew just what to say and when. "I love you, Audie." She could now say those words without fear. "C'mon." Olivia looped her arm through Audra's. "Let's go. I have a wedding to get to."

While waiting for his bride, Erik tugged at his tailed tuxedo. Today, he was marrying the woman of his dreams. The day his mother had bought the gown, she'd told him that Olivia looked like Cinderella in it. At that moment, Erik decided he would give her a true fairytale wedding. He couldn't wait to see Olivia's face when she saw the setting that he, Aunt Adell, and his mother had come up with. It blessed him that Olivia trusted him so completely with the details.

On this warm June evening, under God's canopy of stars, they would be married at precisely 9:00 PM. Erik wanted it to be midnight, but his mother talked him out of it saying, no one would come. He relented. With the help of some men from church, they had built an oblong platform, with three steps leading up to it. The passageway onto it resembled a castle. Only it was just a front. He'd gotten the idea from a renaissance fair he'd gone to one time during a family vacation in Colorado. It served him well now.

At the bottom of each step, on the side was a tall,

specially ordered courting candle, identical to the one he'd given to Olivia. A tall, lit candle with a white ribbon flowed down the length of it. The platform had lattice sides, three feet from the floor with a flat rail on top. Each had hundreds of white lights, greenery and white roses. Seven spindly, lit courting candles were spaced evenly on the flat rail.

The spindle poles and lattice roof of the structure were covered with greenery, white roses, and tiny white lights.

White lattice walls encased the perimeter of their wedding site. The walls matched the stage walls with greenery, lights, and roses. Placed on the neatly mowed grass, were rows and rows of white wooden backed chairs with crushed navy blue velvet seats, filled to capacity with wedding guests.

And now, any moment his bride would enter under a white lattice archway mingled with greenery, light blue and dark blue lights, and make her way up to him on the wooden floor covered with light and dark blue glass tiles. At that moment, it would all be perfect.

Erik's insides shook when his dad signaled from the back that his bride was on her way.

♥♥♥

"Lands o' Goshen!" Olivia blurted when she stepped outside her cottage and saw Adell, Camara, and Mrs. Cole sitting on one side of an open, horse-drawn carriage. Tears stung the back of her eyes, but she refused to cry. She didn't want red, puffy eyes for her wedding.

"Come on, Livvy!" Audra called as she bounced to the carriage.

A coachman helped Audra up and then Olivia.

"Erik asked me to tie this around your eyes. He didn't want you to see the surprise until you get there." Camara handed the long silk strip to Audra.

She wrapped it around Olivia's head, covering her eyes, and then helped her friend sit down on the velvet seat.

Then with one quick lurch, they were off. The sound of horse's hooves clicking on the pavement ticked away the minutes until they stopped.

The carriage shifted. Olivia waited while the others got out.

"Your turn now, Miss."

She reached for his hand, and the coachman helped her down and guided her about ten steps before stopping.

"Okay, you can remove your blindfold now," Camara said.

Olivia untied the silk. When it fell away, her mouth opened and her eyes widened. This time she was truly speechless. And this time she couldn't stop the tears.

With her wedding party surrounding her, she stared at the breathtaking sight. This surpassed all of her wildest dreams.

Her eyes locked on Erik standing solidly at the end of that aisle, and love, unlike any she'd known before, surged through her. The question on his face melted her heart. How could he even wonder if she liked it? She loved it! Olivia sent him her brightest smile ever and nodded.

Pure pleasure lit up his face and her heart even more

than all the thousands of tiny lights around her could. Her groom was as handsome, if not handsomer, than any prince, in any movie, she'd ever seen. And to think she thought fairytales couldn't come true. Well, hers was about to.

Then beyond the thousands of lights, she saw it. She shook her head and laughed. Behind the renaissance platform, looking totally out of place stood the Mad Masher. Leave it to Erik. It was so him. She looked back at him, and his grin said it all.

If it wasn't for that monster truck they might have never met. Well, that and the Lord. God had definitely turned what the devil had meant for her destruction into something good. Something very, very good.

After Mrs. Cole was seated, Adell walked down the walkway and stood on the bottom step opposite of Erik's brother Tony.

Next was Camara, who stood on the second step from the bottom, opposite of Chase.

Then Audra, who stood on the first step, opposite of Erik's brother, Slick.

The tiered wedding party was in place. Now it was her turn.

A violin player, a guitarist, and a flute player joined together in perfect harmony. Sweet music floated over her already heightened senses. She looped her arm through Audra's dad's arm.

"I'm so happy for you, Olivia," Mr. Darron said, looking down at her with a smile, and somehow, she felt as if her parents were right there with her as well.

Too touched with emotion to speak, she nodded.

With each slow step she took forward, she fought the urge to pick up her skirt and run toward Erik. After all the heartache she'd endured in her lifetime, she didn't want to waste even one more moment of precious time.

At the bottom of the stairs, Erik stepped forward, his love-filled eyes never leaving hers. When Mr. Darron gave her away, Erik extended his hand toward her, and she laid her hand in his. Her groom looped her arm through his, and together they walked up the steps.

Facing the love of her life, she said her vows. And when they got to the part of till death do you part, no fear accompanied those words. She was married to the man of her dreams. The man who promised to love her and to cherish her forever. Her very own Prince Charming. God had indeed taken what was meant for evil and had turned it into something good. Only good didn't begin to describe what was happening to her.

"You may now kiss the bride."

And he did.

With their lips and hearts joined, Olivia's soul rejoiced. Déjà vu had never felt so good.

But as for you, you meant evil against me,
but God meant it for good.

—Genesis 50:20a

Other Books by Debra Ullrick

Groom Wanted

It's a perfect plan-best friends Leah Bowen and Jake Lure will each advertise for mail-order spouses in the papers, and then Jake will help select Leah's future husband, while Leah picks Jake's bride-to-be! Surely the ads will find them what they seek: a wife who'll appreciate Jake's shy charm and a groom who'll take Leah away from the Idaho Territory she detests.

When the responses to the postings pour in, it seems all Leah's and Jake's dreams will soon come true. But the closer they each get to the altar, the less appealing marrying a stranger becomes. Is it too late to turn back-or to turn around and find the happiness they truly seek together, at last?

The Unexpected Bride

After the disaster of his first marriage, Haydon Bowen has no intention of marrying again. Unfortunately, his brother has some intentions of his own, and plans to see to it that Haydon finds happiness once more. So he answers a "groom wanted" advertisement—in Haydon's name—and sends Haydon to meet his new bride at the stagecoach stop!

For beautiful, cultured Rainelle Devonwood, any dangers she may face in the Idaho Territories are preferable to staying with her abusive brother. So even when Rainee learns she's a mistakenly ordered bride, she won't let Haydon drive her away. She's up to the challenge of life on the difficult, demanding frontier...and the great challenge of opening Haydon's heart again.

The Unlikely Wife

The arrival of Michael Bowen's bride, married sight unseen by proxy, sends the rancher reeling. With her trousers, cowboy hat and rifle, she looks like a female outlaw—not the genteel lady he corresponded with for months. He's been hoodwinked into marriage with the wrong woman!

Selina Farleigh Bowen loved Michael's letters, even if she couldn't read them herself. A friend read them to her, and wrote her replies—but apparently that "friend" left things out, like Michael's dream of a wife who was nothing like her. Selina won't change who she is, not even for the man she loves. Yet time might show Michael the true value of his unlikely wife.

A Log Cabin Christmas

A New York Times & CBA Bestseller

Experience Christmas through the eyes of adventuresome settlers who relied on log cabins built from trees on their own land to see them through the cruel forces of winter. Discover how rough-hewed shelters become a home in which faith, hope, and love can flourish. Marvel in the blessings of Christmas celebrations without the trappings of modern commercialism where the true meaning of the day shines through. And treasure this exclusive collection of nine Christmas romances penned by some of Christian fiction's best-selling authors.

The Unintended Groom
Colorado Courtship
Reunited at Christmas
Christmas Belles of Georgia
Dixie Hearts
The Bride Wore Coveralls
A Dozen Apologies
Forewarned
Catch Me If You Can (Sequel to Déjà vu Bride)

Visit the author's website:
www.DebraUllrick.com

About the Author

Debra Ullrick is a hot rod, figure-eight races, classic cars, mud-boggin', monster trucks fanatic, who loves Jesus. Her hobbies include, going to classic car auto shows, collecting muscle car and monster truck models, reading, writing, drawing western art, feeding wild birds, playing with her Manx cat Tickles, visiting with family and friends, surfing the Internet, watching movies, especially every available version of Jane Austen's stories, Monster Jam World Finals DVD's, Ma and Pa Kettle, Little People, Big World, CASTLE, COPS, and the PBS documentaries, Frontier House, 1900's house, and Manor House.

Debra and her real-life hero of forty years, along with their now married daughter lived and worked on cattle ranches in the Colorado Rocky Mountains until a few years ago. Now they live down in the flatlands where they're still experiencing cultural whiplash from big city living.

Her debut novel, *The Bride Wore Coveralls,* the first book in this series is available through **www.amazon.com** and numerous other places on the Internet.

Debra loves to hear from her readers.

To contact her visit her website at **www.debraullrick.com** or write her at **christianromancewriter@gmail.com.** You can find Debra on **Twitter** and **Facebook**.

Sweet Impressions
PUBLISHING

www.ingramcontent.com/pod-product-compliance
Lightning Source LLC
Chambersburg PA
CBHW022201170626
46807CB00005B/2296